SECRETS OF THE

FALL

kailin gow

A New Adult/Contemporary Adult Loving
Summer Novel

Secrets of the Fall (Donovan Brothers #2: Loving Summer #3)

Secrets of the Fall

Published by THE EDGE

THE EDGE is an imprint of Sparklesoup Inc.

Copyright © 2013 Kailin Gow

For information, please contact:

THE EDGE at Sparklesoup

1·252 Culver Dr., A732

Irvine, CA 92604

www.theEdgeBooks.com

First Edition.

Printed in the United States of America.

ISBN: 978-1-59748-076-5

Prologue

Nat's Letter to Summer

My Perfect Summer,

I know we're used to calling or texting each other whenever we needed to talk to each other, but I wanted to try something different this time, because this is one of those times that I wish to preserve in memory, as well as paper in hopes that someday our children or future generation could read and cherish.

Aunt Sookie had always been fond of letters, written in the old fashioned way. That when forced to sit down to write a letter, taking pen to paper, you spend more time thinking about what you want to say, and how to say it.

She told me once that traditions like that are worth preserving. And when it comes to anything to do with you, I want to make sure it is preserved.

Aunt Sookie lived life to the fullest. She taught us to learn from the past, enjoy the now, and prepare for the future. You have always been part of my past, my now, and even my future.

I have avoided love for so long. I have been too afraid to open myself up to it, afraid I will only be disappointed. But when you came along into my life, so new to the world at only four years old to my five years old, I felt the stirrings of love and friendship. It wasn't until we were beginning our teens that the love I felt for you was the kind a man has for a woman.

My instructions to you when you're ready to read this letter is to live life to the fullest. To love life to the fullest. Regardless of who you end up with, who is blessed to be the man to spend the rest of your life with, I wish you happiness. And a lifetime of lasting love.

Wherever you go, whatever the weather and time of year; with you, it'll always be a Perfect Summer.

I love you with all my heart.

Your Nat in Shining Armor

<u>Summer</u>

I've read Nat's letter to me again today. Two weeks after finding out he had gone missing. Two whole freaking weeks. It felt like a lifetime when all you've been doing was crying and drowning in incredible indescribable pain.

No, actually I did more than cry…I nearly lost my mind.

I never thought missing someone could hurt so much. When Aunt Sookie died and left me alone to live at her Malibu beach house, known as the "Pad" and to manage her acting academy, I was in shock, but I was able to manage. Somehow. Somewhere inside of me, there was a strength that I could draw from, instilled by Aunt Sookie herself, that gave me hope that I can make it through. There was grief no doubt, but I did managed to pull myself together enough to finish high school, get a volleyball scholarship to USC and on an early admissions, and run the acting school Aunt Sookie had left me to run.

To go on living my life day to day.

To get up and out of bed, to brush my teeth, get dressed, and go on about my day like it was just another day.

I could manage.

Because it was what Aunt Sookie had taught me to do. To carry on. Aunt Sookie had asked me, had made me promise that I would carry on. Just like Nat had asked me to do in his last letter to me…before he disappeared.

Before I got word from Drew that Nat had not returned from his life and death mission.

The thought was in back of everyone's mind, but we didn't want to say it aloud. Nat had gone to Afghanistan on a rescue mission to find and bring back his father, the billionaire tycoon of Donovan Dynamics, who was there for a secret security mission. The danger was immense, and if Nat and Mr. Donovan did not return, chances were they weren't going to.

It was the hardest thing I've ever face…more so than the cyber-attacks or even the near attempts on my life by the stalker, because with Nat gone, it was as though a large part of me went missing, too. I didn't know this at the time, but loving Nat had been the most constant thing I've had throughout my life. I've always loved him, but when we finally got together physically, it was as though a part of me had awaken. When he and I finally made love, I became further attached to Nat in so many ways. He really was my knight in shining armor. My pirate to my princess in the fairy tale play Aunt Sookie had cast us in when we were little.

When Aunt Sookie died and I had to take over running the school, take over taking care of myself and managing all of Aunt Sookie's bills, the Pad, and everything else she was involved in, I had to grow up overnight. I wasn't the same Summer Jones as I was the last summer Aunt Sookie was alive. I wasn't the sweet and naïve girl I was who stayed with her aunt during the summers and then school year while her mother traveled the world on military business. I became Summer Jones, college student, owner of Aunt Sookie's Acting Academy, and inheritor of the Pad. Also, thrown into public briefly as hottie actor Astor Fairway's girl. Briefly until we broke up. Me first, and then Astor. That was a whole different story altogether, which maybe someday I will tell…the whole dating Astor Fairway the celebrity thing…but I digress. Sometimes, life could be too much to handle all by yourself. Sometimes, you couldn't be that strong, but have to let go of yourself to fall and get rebuilt again.

Strength came in different ways, and when Aunt Sookie got sick, when the Donovans faced divorce and suicide at their home, we all learned that strength came from helping each other and standing by each other when the going got tough. So when Nat, who had always been my rock, went missing on his mission to find his father, I went ballistic. Sobbed for days, didn't eat or sleep for days, missed classes, and even refused to crawl out of bed.

It was too much to handle. Missing Nat and wondering if he would ever come back, chewed me up inside and out…screaming about it, crying about it could not take away the pain enough.

So I did the best I could and turned to my friend who had always been there for me, too. Someone who knew what I was going through, who was close to Nat and loved him too. I turned to the only other rock in my life and fell into his arms. And now…it was more complicated than ever.

Secrets of the Fall (Donovan Brothers #2: Loving Summer #3)

I glanced over at the tanned bare chest of the naked man next to me in bed. Even in the early morning grey light of Southern California fog, he had one of the most impressive body I've seen. I'd be lying if I said I wasn't attracted to him at least one bit. Any girl who had eyes would be.

He opened his beautiful blue ones and stared lovingly at me while I took him all in.

"Hi Beautiful," he said, reaching a finger to brush a strand of my long chestnut hair behind my ear. He smiled his slow sexy smile that revealed his straight white teeth. My breath caught in my throat. He really was that good-looking...the guy who modeled those underwear ads, that guy who had random girls stopping him on the streets or at supermarkets to give him their numbers...that guy was Drew Donovan...Nat's younger brother.

The guy who made hot passionate love to me last night when he came over and found me sobbing in the bathtub with Nat's letter in my hands. And a razor nearby.

Drew Donovan had saved my life last night.

It wasn't the first time he had saved my life, but this time, it was the first time I succumbed to my feelings for him, and it made everything much more complicated.

Chapter 1

<u>Drew</u>

It takes a major screw up to fuck up a situation even further than it could be.

Me making love to Summer at her most vulnerable was a major screw up.

Did I regret it? Part of me wished it didn't happen under those circumstances...that Summer had wanted me to make love to her because she loved me and wanted me for myself, and not as Nat's stand-in.

The other part of me, which you could imagine which, was loving Summer a whole lot more. There were no regrets there.

And judging by the way Summer responded, she

enjoyed it immensely.

Was it good? The question should be…how could it not be? When you're making love to a woman you cherish, and all you want to do is make her feel good, how could it not be good?

Talking about it almost cheapens the experience. To me, making love to Summer for the first time, was mind-blowing. I'd go to hell and back for her because she's that woman for me. She's the woman who can launch wars…my Helen of Troy. She's the queen who can bring powerful men to their knees…my Cleopatra. She is the woman who helped me reach my potential, the woman who saw through my bullshit, called me out on it, and still loved me for all my flaws and imperfections. All packaged up nicely in a killer Victoria Secret model body with a wicked sense of justice.

As always, when Summer walks into a room, she brings all the sunshine in, no matter how dark it is. Even when I found her sobbing in the bathtub with Nat's letter in her hands and a razor blade nearby; there was still a thread of hope within her that made it possible for me to push that razor blade away, take her into my arms, and kiss the tears away, and have her come back to me.

"Summer!" I shook her in the middle of her bedroom. "Don't even think about it," I scolded her while desperately kissing her lips, her cheeks, and her eyelids. "I'm here. I'm here for you. Please, don't do this to yourself. Please don't hurt yourself."

Summer's naked body was whacked with sobs as she realized what she was about to do. "Oh, Drew," she cried. "This hurts. It hurts so much. What am I going to do? I don't know…"

"Dammit, Summer," I said almost angrily. "Don't you dare leave me, too." I held her tight against my chest, not caring that her wet skin and hair was soaking through my t-shirt. "Don't you pull a Nat on me and leave, Summer. I need you. I miss Nat, too, but I so desperately…" I kissed her on the mouth hungrily now, my tongue dipping in to taste her tongue as I press hard against her soft wet body, kissing her with all that I have, trying hard to get through to her, trying hard to make her feel something…anything…so

- 14 -

that she can feel me alive with her. "I'm here, Summer. I am here in the flesh. I know you can feel me. I know you can touch and taste me. In the flesh…for you. I'm here for you, and you can have me. Any way you want me. Summer. I'm yours. I. Desperately…" my hands cupped her smooth firm but round butt and press my jeans-clad crotch against her. "Need you."

I was full-on devouring her mouth and making my way down her neck and shoulders when I stopped and took a look at her. She was standing still with her big hazel eyes staring straight at me…her lips glistening and slightly open from my kisses. Oh God, I wanted to dip right in again and take her mouth fully in mine and kiss the living breath out of her. Despite this situation of finding her in her bathtub, I found myself hotter for her than ever. I've never seen her more vulnerable, and it brought out my most primal urge to protect her, comfort her, and do everything I could to make her feel safe again.

"Drew," she said calmly, her tears drying on her cheeks. She reached up a finger to touch my cheeks softly and gently. I stared at her, mesmerized by her calmness as she leaned in towards me. I think I even held my breath as she stared into my eyes briefly before leaning in to kiss my cheeks with her soft sexy lips. She kissed one cheek and then the other before raising her eyes to look into mine again. That look of intensity in her eyes. That look of desire mixed with vulnerability, nearly made me lose all control. I wanted to grab her and carry her off to bed. "Drew," she said again, calmly and softly. "Don't cry, too. I'm here. I'm still here."

It hit me then that I had been crying when I found her in the tub, grabbed her out of it, and began kissing her furiously and desperately. I didn't even realize I had been crying, I was so lost in trying to save Summer from taking her own life.

The thought of losing her at that moment caused something in me to break, to lose all my inhibitions, and to just be me at my most rawest, my most primal self…with Summer. I didn't care about my image as a walking one-night stand. I didn't care about football. I didn't care about anything about me. All I cared about was Summer. She was what mattered. Nothing else.

I knew then that I had to tell her. I had to let Summer know how much she meant to me. No more playing games. No more being friend-zoned. I desperately wanted her. I desperately loved her, more than my own life.

She needed to know how much she meant to me. She needed to know that if she took her own life and left me standing there alone, I could never recover from it. "Summer," I said, my voice shaking with emotion. If I cried, I didn't care. Getting her to understand I wanted her to live was more important than any stupid male macho crap. I was suddenly that little boy at Aunt Sookie's Malibu pad along with my twin sister Rachel, playing with and crushing on cute little Summer when we were little. I was the boy who watched Summer grow into a beauty every summer, while being able to joke around, swim with, and even run along the beach with. She was the only girl besides Rachel whom I cared about other than as a sexual conquest. So now here she was, naked, vulnerable, beautifully wild, and looking at me with a look that melted me.

"You're the only girl who can make me cry like that, Summer. You're the only girl who can see straight through me and into my heart. If I lost you, I don't know what I'd do. You are my lifeline to sanity, my window of hope. If you dare attempt to do what you were thinking of doing, you may as well kill me, too."

Summer's eyes widen as she gasped and took a deep breath in. "No, no, Drew," she cried, shaking her head. "This isn't about you. It's about me, but no. I would never want to hurt you like that. Oh God...what was I thinking? I wasn't thinking...I don't know what got into me...I'm sorry."

I took her hands and held them tightly in my own. "I swear Summer, if you even attempt to do what you were thinking of doing, you've signed my death warrant, too. Think about that. If you go, you're taking me down with you. I will not let you do it. Because no matter how bleak it may seem, no matter how far you've fallen, there is always hope. There is always another way. Believe me, I had been there before...and then you realize that when you've hit rock bottom, that it's a good thing. There's nowhere else to go but up. You may not see it now, but you will."

I took her hands and begin kissing her knuckles. "A few months ago, I was having such dark dreams that it scared me. I never thought I would, but then it crept up on me, and I was suddenly feeling all these emotions. I was on the brink, but then something happened."

Summer looked at me and her eyes filled with unshed tears. "What?"

"I thought of you...how you may need me one day. How I wanted to be there for you. I thought of Rachel, who would no longer have a brother. I thought of Nat, who needed me to help him deal with Mom and Dad. I thought of Mom, who needed all of us to pull through for her. I even thought of my asshole cheating father. I even thought of Aunt Sookie, and how much she enjoyed life to the fullest. How she lived her short life to the fullest with no regrets. If I left, if I had given up, I would have so many regrets, Summer. And one of the most biggest regrets I'll ever have is that I never got to experience, not took a chance on loving you."

I took a deep jagged breath and continued while Summer covered her mouth with her hands, overcome with emotions. "You have me, Summer. And I have you. When the going gets tough, I'll always be here for you." I kissed her fully on the mouth. "I'll always be here for you because Summer…as much as I've been fighting it, as much as I've tried to stay away, I can't. I love you. I love you so much that just the thought of you not being in my life, broke me."

"Drew…I," Summer began with tears rolling down her cheeks again but I captured her mouth with mine as my tongue tangled with hers.

She moaned a deep moan before I deepen the kiss and wrapped my arms around her small waist, lifting her so that her legs straddled my waist. Oh heavenly mother of God, I could not stop myself then, just feeling her naked skin and her open warm core pressed against me. There were times when we were naked or heavily making out before, but this time was different. This time, I felt as though if I didn't have her, if I didn't show her how much I loved her, it would be a matter of life and death. Literally.

Kailin Gow

"Summer..." I began, but she hushed me while raking her fingers through my hair.

"Drew...you are all I have now. I'm sorry for scaring you like that. I am so messed up right now, and Nat's not even here, and I..."

"Hush," I said, cupping her chin with my hand and lifting her face up to meet my gaze. "Like I said, I'm here now and I'll do anything to help make your pain go away. Anything, Summer, especially my body. Do what you will with me. Everything I have is yours."

"Your what?" Summer asked almost incredulously.

"My body," I repeated, a little huskier this second knowing how it was more of a benefit to me than to Summer, actually. Damn, I wanted her body to do with it as I so pleased.

"If it can ease your pain and fill that void of missing Nat, Summer, I want you to pretend I'm Nat, use me, use my body as though I was Nat, to help you not miss him so badly." As soon as I said this, I felt a pang of regret. It was like that one time Summer wanted to experience no-holds

- 21 -

bar casual sex just to know how meaningless it was. To her it was meaningless, but to me…giving her Drewgasms (pleasuring her with everything I've got except without me going all the way) made it painful for me. She thought it was meaningless, but I fell deeper and deeper in love with her. She once said she couldn't have sex with anyone without it meaning something. I once thought it was just something I like doing as part of me being a guy. But all that's changed. The tables have been turned. I was now the one who needed more. So, as soon as the word was out about my offer for her to use my body as a substitute for Nat just so she can get over missing him, I knew I was going to lose my heart once more to her…hard.

"You mean it?" Summer asked.

"Yes," I said. "I want you to get it out of your system, and to be able to rely on me to do whatever it takes to get you through it." *Even if I was going to end up having my heart broken for it.*

"No attachments then?" Summer asked. "I can't handle getting attached like that to anyone again. I can't let myself get as attached to Nat as I was."

I felt myself tense up. As much as my body craved Summer, I still wanted everything else with her. Everything including her attachment and her love for me.

I was about to change my mind and tell her it probably wasn't a good idea when Summer grabbed my t-shirt, rolled it off me, and began kissing my chest. Just looking at her, naked, hot, and full of desire in her eyes made me instantly forget my protest. She taking charge like this ignited my most primal urge as a man, and I grabbed her by her waist, turned her around and flung her onto bed. With frantic hands, I unbuckled my belt, unbuttoned my jeans, and slipped it off. I wasn't even wearing underwear today, which brought a smile to my face when I noticed Summer's surprised expression.

"You really have earned your rep as a ladies' man," she joked.

"What ladies' man?" I said, sliding on top of her, my heated flesh against hers. The movement had us both take in a breath, it felt so good. I kissed her breasts and then licked her skin down to her very core, where I worked her with my tongue and fingers until she was crying out my name as one Drewgasm after another whacked her tantalizing body. I moved up to kiss her face and her lips, positioning myself up against her and loving how I was able to rub up against her. After some intense kissing and pleasuring, I cupped her face in my hands before I said, "I love you, Summer. My God, I want you."

She looked into my eyes with unwavering clarity and said, "I want you too."

That was all it took for me to ease myself into her, plunging deep into her before we both succumbed to rocking each other to the point of release.

Oh man, was it worth the wait.

I've had countless numbers of girls before, but none of them compared to what I've experienced with Summer then. It was not just a physical connection, but an intense emotional one filled with passionate and deep love. I saw the sky explode before my eyes, and felt a tremor go through my entire body. I was in awe of her. I could not believe I was holding, kissing, and making love to the girl I've been in love with since I could remember ever knowing what a girl was.

As much as I loved the sex, I knew if I continued on, and if she didn't feel the same about me, I would be the one sitting in a tub with the razor blade nearby. Making love to her fully and finally, meant the world and more to me.

After making love to her tonight, I would be devastated if she didn't end up picking me, and being my girl. If she ends up going back to Nat or choosing that pretty boy Astor over me, I really would go nuts.

I squeezed my eyes shut in guilt and frustration. I could kick myself for feeling the way I was feeling at this moment. Nat had been missing for two weeks now, and tonight was the only time I was glad he wasn't home.

Because all I wanted...all I could think about was having Summer all to myself and doing anything I could to make that happen.

Chapter 2

<u>Drew</u>

I decided to drive Summer and me in my blue Lexus up the California coastline from Malibu to San Francisco instead of taking the corporate jet for our first board meeting at Donovan Dynamics. With Dad gone, Nat missing, and Mother of questionable sound mind; I was the one Nat and my father had put in charge of to represent the interests of the family for the company. Nat had also asked Summer to help me out with the responsibility…something I was definitely grateful for. Summer had a good head on her shoulders despite the recent incidence in her bathtub. She was young, but she's already spent years helping Aunt

Sookie run a school. What she lacked in experience, she made up for with her loyalty to the Donovans and having our best interests in mind.

I glanced over at Summer, who was wearing a cotton and lace white summer dress, that showed off her tanned skin, had a tapered waistline that tucked in her small waist while pushing up her breasts. She wasn't overly large, but her mango-sized breasts looked like they could pop out at any moment, the way they sat in that push up bra kind of style top. I wanted to stop driving and dip my head into that glorious cleavage of hers and suck on each breast, her breasts were so enticing to me.

Her hair was swept off her face with a gemstone barrette at her crown, while the rest of her long chestnut waves fell softly down her shoulders. A light dusting of golden tan colored her skin, and the pink blush she wore high on her cheekbones brought out her pretty cheeks. She was so beautiful, I just wanted to stare at her all day.

It was Monday, and just two days ago, I was over at her house, checking in on her when I found her in the bathtub. Just two days ago, we had made love for the first time. I haven't been able to get her taste and how she felt clenched around me out of my head since. I wanted to spend as much time as I could around her, but because of this trip, I had to go to football practice the next day, practice all day, and then rush back to my apartment, pack, and get ready for my trip back home to San Francisco. Meanwhile, Summer seemed much better so she went to the Academy, taught a class, and did whatever she planned on doing. I didn't ask. I was just glad she was acting better.

"So, Drew," Summer said, relaxing into the soft leather seat. "Why the drive instead of taking the jet as always?" She looked down at her dress, her high-heeled wedge sandals, and her small clutch purse. "Had I known we were going to be on the road for, let's see…five to six hours, I would have worn a t-shirt and jeans. And sneakers!" She bent down and took off her sandals. "These shoes are pretty, but they're killing my feet."

I laughed. I should have known Summer would be practical like that. "We can stop at a restaurant or motel and you can change," I said, glancing over at her. "I figure it would be nice to go for a drive. You know, clears the head, take in some of that nice fresh air."

"That's it?" Summer asked, taking off her other sandal and pulling her legs up to nestle on the seat. "You enjoy driving?"

"Sometimes," I said. "I like it when I want to clear my head." I thought about my long distance drive from San Francisco to Malibu that one time I was so upset about seeing Nat and Summer together. If it hadn't been for the drive and me needing to get to Malibu, I may have done something drastic and even tragic. I was the one who felt like I was falling down to rock bottom back then.

But, as I mentioned, since I did drive, by the time I reached Malibu, I had some time to think and to calm down. I no longer felt so vulnerable and angry. Instead I realized in clear details what I had to do. Step away from Nat and Summer so we were just friends. To me, Summer's heart was still with Nat, and I just couldn't compete so I didn't, and I ended up stepping away.

Secrets of the Fall (Donovan Brothers #2: Loving Summer #3)

"So," Summer asked, her body turned towards me to give me all her attention. "What could you possibly have in that head of yours, that requires spending 5 to 6 hours to clear?" She smiled her big sunny smile. Gosh I missed it. I haven't seen her smile like that since she heard the news about Nat.

I thought about everything…school, my football scholarship, Mom, Dad, Rachel, running Aunt Sookie's Academy, Nat, Donovan Dynamics, and mostly of Summer. Was she alright or was she pretending to be this cheerful?

"Shoot," she said, crossing her arms. "Tell me, Drew. I know we've both been so busy with everything, and we see each other all the time, but when we get together, we never have the chance to talk…just talk, like we used to during summers."

"Summer," I said, taking a deep breath and exhaling it. I leaned in to whisper in her ear. As I did, her hair brushed against my nose, and I paused for a second. She smelled like a warm ocean breeze mixed with sweet vanilla. "Ummm," I growled instinctively. "You smell good enough to eat." My voice was husky, and I had to swallow. Without thinking, I took my right hand off the steering wheel and instinctively cupped her chin, turning her head towards me. My mouth captured her mouth hungrily, and I used my tongue to trace the inner outline of her lips.

This time, Summer groaned, while kissing me back harder.

I was lost in her kiss. One night alone with her making love was not going to satisfy me...instead, it just made me want her more.

"Bahhhhh!"

A truck honked loudly at us, as I brought both hands back to the steering wheel and turned, avoiding side-swiping that truck.

I quickly re-adjusted the car, and kept driving. After taking a shaky breath, I looked over at Summer. She had gone white.

"Summer?" I asked. "Are you okay? We're fine now. The truck missed us. What's the matter, baby? It's okay, okay."

I had to pull her into my arms, but I couldn't while driving. I had to wrap my arms around her, hold on tightly and make sure Summer felt safe again. Gosh this woman brings out the most primal man in me. I didn't waste any time pulling off the road and heading onto a side street where there was one or two restaurants. Summer had to change out of her clothes, and I wanted something to eat. Perfect, we could do all this at Carlos Cantina and Grill.

As soon as I pulled into the parking lot of the somewhat large restaurant and killed the engine, I grabbed Summer's hands. "Hey, Summer," I said gently. "What's the matter? You okay?"

Summer nodded, but I can see her body trembling slightly.

"Fuck it," I unbuckled my seat belt, got out of the car, walked over to her side, opened the door, and grabbed her. She was surprised at first, especially since I was able to

Kailin Gow

lift her up easily and carry her like a caveman into the Grill, her legs dangling while I held her around her waist.

A bunch of patrons looked surprised when I walked in, holding this gorgeous woman in my arms. I think Summer was too stunned to even talk.

"Need a booth?" the hostess asked.

I nodded.

She led us to a spacious one hidden in the dark corner of the restaurant. "Your server will be right with you," she said.

"Thank you," I muttered, still focused on Summer. The tension between her, especially with me holding her against my body like this, with her boobs practically falling out because of the tilt forward, was so thick, I could cut it with a steak knife. My jeans were straining with the added tightness of my extremely aroused member I called Little Drew.

I laid Summer gently down on the padded seat of the booth, slid in and kissed her gently on the mouth before moving down to her neck and collar bone. "Can you tell me what just happened?" I asked between kisses.

Summer didn't respond back, while I continued to kiss her, caress her with my tongue, and move my hand up and down her thigh.

"Could you feel me, Summer?" I asked. "Could you let me know how you're doing, even if you can't talk?"

Summer barely nodded, but I can see her body responding to my touch and kisses. Whatever it takes to snap her out of this, I'll do.

After some more heated kisses, I reached under the table to travel underneath her skirt to touch her intimately. When you're with the woman you love, and you think she's the most beautiful person in the world, it's natural for you to want to touch her every chance you get. "You know what I want to do with you, don't you?" I asked. "Just say the word, and I can find us a place." Was she missing Nat? Was she missing Aunt Sookie? I wished I could get through to her. I wished she would talk to me. For the first time in my life, instead of wanting to fuck Summer hard in every way I can imagine, I just wanted her to talk to me. Of course, if she wanted me to fuck her hard, I'd do that, too.

"I want..." Summer began.

My ears perked up like I was some kind of dog in heat. Man, Summer had me whipped. But boy, did I want it. It would be a privilege for me to be whipped and bound by her. Not that I think she would be into that, but if she wanted to try it, I would try anything with her. I'd do anything with her, for her. I'd even wait for her.

She closed her eyes for a second and opened them wide, the gold specks in them shining bright into mine. I could get lost in those eyes. "I want...to move on. I want some closure. Oh God, when the truck came at us, I thought we were going to die. Then I saw Nat's face flash by, and I knew I have to find out what happened to him no matter what. I need to know or I will have the deepest regret..."

I took her hands in mine and squeezed them. "Done. We will look into this and try our darn hardest to find Nat, when we get to San Fran. It's one of the reasons why we're heading there in the first place."

"Good," Summer said with a smile. "I just have this deep sense that Nat is still alive."

With the windy road along the cliffs and the view of the blue ocean below, the drive was known to be pretty romantic, although Little Drew as still there, and I was having the hardest time concentrating on the road.

Chapter 3

Summer

We arrived at Donovan Dynamics hours later and parked in the parking lot, resting for a bit before we had to get out of the car to meet the team. Drew drove like a madman, as eager as I was to get into town, and I was sure he needed a breather before having to face the security team's news about Nat and Mr. Donovan.

After I told Drew about my belief that Nat was still alive, it sank deep into both of our brains that time was of essence to find him, if he was still alive. There wasn't time to waste, and if we wanted to bring him home safe and sound, we have to act fast.

Drew surprised me, too. I thought he would fully take advantage of Nat not being here, but he didn't. He respectfully followed what I wanted. He didn't push, he didn't force the issue. He made me feel as though I was in charge. It was my decision to take the initiative for whatever happened between us.

What happened between us?

My skin heated up when I think about it, and my stomach did flip flops. Then I thought about his large hands touching me at my most private center, his hot mouth kissing every part of me. I could not stay dry and unaffected when it came to Drew. He was Lust personified. Every woman and non-straight man I know would want to experience what it was like to be with Drew. My entire body still shivered from the memory of reaching an orgasm, no a Drewgasm, from him. I swear, the man probably studied enough sex tapes to know where to hit the spot exactly, how to bring women to multiple orgasms, and how to give women the best mind-blowing tonguing in life.

My body and mind (because I love him so much too) was confused with everything that happened between us. We made love. Wild, passionate, unbridled love that came from years of wanting, of desiring a person you couldn't have. We made love like our life depended on it, and despite me telling him it was only casual (since that was what Drew was into, not some kind of commitment), my entire mind, body, and soul was into it. As much as I missed Nat, loved Nat, and wanted him back with me; I could not deny that I wanted Drew with a passion that scared me to death.

From the looks of it, from Drew not being able to stop touching me, brushing up against me, softly touching my shoulders, patting my knee, or even little almost-there warm whispers into my ear; Drew felt the same way.

But I loved Nat, and I couldn't commit to Drew fully if I knew Nat was here. If he was here, I'd finally confront my confused feelings and decide once and for all how to deal with loving both of the Donovan brothers. It was so hard. I've known them for so long, and I know they are both a major part of me. Two parts of one confused but well-loved coin. Being sandwiched between two hot brothers like the Donovans was an impossible situation, but one that I wouldn't trade my life for. But my mind…it was affecting me with guilt, doubts, jealousy, and insecurity. I wasn't the same Summer Jones who had no worries or cares about boys when Aunt Sookie was alive. I was now this confused, emotional, and on-the-brink of a meltdown girl. If Drew hadn't found me in my bathtub sobbing as I re-read Nat's letter to me, ready to end it to escape my pain, I wouldn't be here today, sitting next to Drew, the hottest man on earth, waiting for him to announce that we were here…at Donovan Dynamics where hopefully we could get some answers on Nat and maybe some closure so I could move on, carry on, as painful as it was…with life and everyone I knew in it. Including Drew.

We both got out the car and stood, stretching from the long drive. Then Drew came over to my side and leaned against the car right next to me. "You sure you don't want to stop by my place?" he asked, turning his direct blue eyes to me. He had been driving non-stop for four hours, and I could see the strain in them. "We can rest up a bit, eat, get unpacked, change…"

"Is it far from here?" I asked. The last time I visited Donovan Dynamics, it was with Nat, to meet his team to handle the stalker who had been harassing me. I wasn't paying attention to the distance it was between The Donovan's Nob Hill mansion to Donovan Dynamics.

"Well…" Drew said. "It is a bit of a drive. Not exactly close."

"I'd like to go there to see your mother, check up on her in person, as Nat asked us to, but maybe later?"

"Sure," Drew said, more perceptive than usual. "I know how weird it is right now with you coming over with me, and us seeing Nat's room, my Dad's room and all." Drew raised his hand to his temples. I could see the frustration he had then, as well as all the burden he suddenly inherited with his family. It was a lot for a carefree guy like Drew to take in, and I felt my heart reach out to him.

"Hey Drew, it's okay," I said. "Whatever works is fine with me. If you want to go there first or go to Donovan Dynamics or even just go to a café to relax, I'm fine." I touched his shoulders, and it was as if Drew was brought back into the moment. He smiled a sweet genuinely happy smile with his beautiful blue eyes crinkling.

"If it's alright with you," he said. "I want to spend more time just being with you...no one else."

If my heart was made of butter, it melted then and ran to my knees where I felt the earth shake. Drew, who blew hot and cold, who was never downright sweet on purpose, but cocky and so sure of himself; made my heart melt into a puddle of goo. I don't know if it was because of Nat not being here or because Drew and I became so intimate, but I suddenly had the urge to pull him to me, tippy toe up, and kiss the living daylights out of him.

"Is that what you want?" I smiled, lowering my eyes so he couldn't see how much I wanted it too.

Drew pulled me to him so I was looking up into his chiseled face. His blue eyes bore through me, piercing me in place as though I was hooked onto him by an invisible line. I could drown in those sea-blue eyes. If his eyes drifted off of me, breaking that intense bond we have, I would go crashing down into an ocean of muddled emotions and pattering hearts.

I've loved Drew before, was deadly attracted to him physically and emotionally, but now there was something else, and it scared me. It made me suddenly self-conscious around him.

"You know what I want, Summer," Drew said huskily. "I don't think I'll ever get over this wanting of you." His eyes skimmed my face, and he cupped my chin with one hand while his thumb played with my lower lip. Gosh, that was sensual…him touching my lip like that and looking at me with such hunger.

"So…" I found my voice again, shaking my head so I could think straight. "Wha…"

Drew had entwined his fingers through mine as he pushed me up against the car door. His hips pressed into mine, and I could feel his wanting, feel his heart beating furiously against mine, and taste his lips, slowly, tantalizingly sweet and thorough devouring mine. I moaned a deep throaty moan that got swallowed up by his mouth, but not before Drew gave a low groan.

"I take it," I broke off from between his kisses, "you want to go somewhere else before we go in?"

"Hmm…" Drew muttered, licking the skin behind my ear, his tongue swirling in circles, causing me to shudder.

I wanted to hop onto Drew and straddle my legs around his waist, while pushing him close to my breasts. But then I realized, we were out there in the parking lot, in front of the building. No doubt if anyone looking out the window took a look outside, they would be seeing something close to PG-17 or even R going on. I pulled back. "Drew, we have to go. We can't be doing this right here in front of your family's company building. What must everyone think? They won't take us seriously now."

I was mortified.

But Drew just slowly pulled away and flashed me his signature cocky grin. "Oh, I forgot," he said charmingly. "You see, Summer, when it comes to you, I can't even think straight." He grabbed my hand and reached into the car for my purse, handed it to me, then started leading the way into the steel and glass building taking up the entire block.

"Aren't we going to go somewhere first, freshen up, change?" I asked while walking with him.

"Nope," Drew said as we walked into the impressive lobby with a large waterfall marble sculpture in the center, and headed into an elevator. "I'm as refreshed as I can be…thanks to you," he smirked. When the elevator door closed, he stopped smiling, and his face scrunched up in frustration. "I don't think I can take any more of it…being alone with you without wanting to go further. This…," he said, straightening his white polo shirt and his jeans and indicating the building, "is the distraction I need. Because unless you're willing to go further with me, Summer, I'm having a tough time holding back."

His eyes burned into mine, and I knew he was dead serious.

"How many girls have you had sex with since you told me how you feel about me last summer?" I had to know. Was it just pure sex for him or a lot more? Did we have anything more than this lust we both feel for each other? I knew I lusted after him…my body always respond to him no matter what I was feeling or what my situation, but did we have more than that? Like what I have with Nat?

Drew looked uncomfortable as he shifted his feet. "You know Summer how we weren't together…how I feel about sex…it doesn't mean anything to me."

"Oh?" I couldn't help feeling a little disappointed. So having sex with me didn't mean anything to him?

Drew didn't answer, but ran his fingers through his hair. I took his silence to mean that he had slept with a few girls since he told me he loved me last summer. My heart dropped. I felt as though a rug had been pulled out from under me, but then again…what right did I have to be jealous? I wasn't with him. I still wasn't with him.

"That's the thing, Drew," I said shakily, trying to control my emotions. "With Nat, I never had any doubts where I stood with him…once he told me how he felt about me…I felt secure in knowing he meant it."

"Summer," Drew said urgently. "It's not that I didn't mean it. It's not that I have or haven't slept with anyone since letting you know how I feel about you. It's just…" He threw up his hands and faced me…his face filled with such anguish, love, hurt, and pain. "You're still Nat's girl…in your heart and in person. I could try everything to change that, but deep down, we both know you will always love him." He moved in close to me where his lips almost met mine. "As much as I love Nat, Summer, I want closure, too. For your sake, as well as mine. Because I can't go on loving and wanting you like this, while you love him, too."

I bit my lips and moved a step away from him. Being this physically close to him was clouding my judgment. I knew if I was to make a choice at this moment, I would jump him, and worry about consequences later. If I gave into my feelings and my passion, I would be all over him. I would let him have me through and through. I wanted Drew to ravish me, to use me, to take me. I wanted him to play dirty with me, to bring out the wild side in me.

Secrets of the Fall (Donovan Brothers #2: Loving Summer #3)

I wanted him to bring me to the edge, to stretch me until I couldn't give any further. I knew there was so much within him, so much that he felt but had to restrain that if we were to completely let go and lose ourselves in each other, we would be utterly and deeply gone. There would not be a Drew or a Summer, but just one entity. That kind of passion and love was dangerous.

I wasn't sure if I wanted to take that leap. I wanted a safety net...and that net had always been Nat. Love with him was safer and expected. I wanted to cry. Why did Nat have to go missing? I loved him more than I've ever loved a man, but now with Drew always around me, having been my hero so many times...I couldn't help having strong intense feelings for him, too.

*****

The door of the elevator opened just in time for me to walk out and seek a far enough distance from Drew. He was temptation...especially one I could not fall for in the midst of the security team we were supposed to be working closely with to help get Nat and Mr. Donovan safely back.

Drew looked a little hurt as he noticed me stepping away from him, creating a distance between us. He didn't have time to say anything though as Timothy Childs, one of the executives I met last time came up to us and shook our hands. Tim, a man in his early 40s with dark wavy hair and grey eyes, talked to Drew for a bit before he turned to me. "Summer," he said. "How's everything? I'm glad you and Drew took down Sloane, but anything else came up?"

I shook my head. I haven't been looking nor have I been on the computer much. Since Nat's news, I was fortunate enough for Astor and sometimes a few other actors Astor rung up to help teach and run the academy. "I tried to avoid looking. I've been too much of a wreck these past couple of weeks. So I couldn't really tell you if anything came up," I answered truthfully.

"That's perfectly fine," Tim said. "In fact, we don't want you to look at any of that. Before Nat left, he had us set up a monitoring system and also a team who manually went in and address any of that, including taking legal action when we have to...all without you needing to get involved."

My mouth flew open in astonishment. "Wow, I never even knew."

"That's what we do," Tim said. "Especially since Nat was so behind it, you're one of our priorities."

"I wouldn't be surprise," Drew said walking up to me and putting his arm around my shoulders to lead me over to a group of people, with Tim following. "Summer," Drew said, friendly and confidently, "I want you to meet the team who is working on international assignments. Top secret highly-classified stuff."

My eyes flew up, realizing how complex Donovan Dynamics really was. Nat did mention to me that they received lots of contracts from the U.S. government and maybe even from other countries. Mr. Donovan had truly built up one of the most impressive internet and intelligence companies I've ever seen. I didn't even think there were any companies out there that could compare to what they could do. No wonder why it was a multi-billion dollars corporation.

But did they have what it takes to get Nat and Mr. Donovan their founders back?

Drew led me into a conference room that looked like any conference rooms I've seen on television. A basic meeting room with tinted glass walls, a large round table in the middle, a white board in front, and a small bar in the back. Nothing too fancy nor too plain. When I walked into the room, the five people sitting around the table stood up.

I glanced over at Drew, and he had a straight business-like face on, completely different than I've ever seen him. "Gentlemen and ladies…" he nodded at some men in their early forties and fifties wearing dark suits and a woman in her late thirties or early forties with sleek auburn hair to her shoulders, red lips, and a grey skirt suit. "This is Summer Jones."

"Hello," I said, feeling self-conscious amongst this group of distinguished-looking people. They all looked like they could be my professors at USC. My hands automatically went to straighten my skirt, but Drew came over, put one arm around my waist and led me to meet and greet each person.

"Summer," he said, "This is Kevin Soboski, Director of International Operations," he said in front of a large man with brown cropped hair and a strong jawline. After greeting Kevin, Drew moved to a medium-sized man slightly balding and wearing glasses named Joseph Conrad. I greeted him and we both mentioned how his name sounded like the classic novelist, but he said he was far from anything literary. He was a techie, and his entire world revolves around high-tech espionage equipment and security systems.

"Robert Frost," a man with spiky grey hair and a large build said with a deep voice. He shook my hand. "Not the poet," he said again, when I opened my mouth to ask. "I handle logistics and sensitive information."

"Hi, I'm Timothy Childs," Tim said. "You already know that. I handle U.S. operations. But I'm helping with coordinating this entire operations."

"Nothing but the best for our boss," the woman said with a deep and firm commanding voice. She came around and shook my hand before crossing her arms and walking to the front to join Drew. "I'm Karen Waters…I'm working with Tim and Kevin with getting clearance, getting documents and everything from the country so we can move in further. In other words, I'm the one handling the details, the legalities so to speak, and the relations."

I stood up straighter while I listened to Karen talked about some of the complexities of the mission. What it was and how Donovan Dynamics got involved. "You see, we got a contract from a Turkish company to help build their company security system. They specifically asked for Mr. Donovan. When he arrived there with a few of our international-based team members, instead of finding a company building, they found an abandoned warehouse."

"It was a set up," Karen went on, "by an international cyberspace crime ring."

"An elaborate setup," Tim added. "We couldn't even detect foul play. Everything checked."

"But as I said," Karen continued. "The entire operations went south. Apparently it was a kidnapping scheme to obtain Mr. Donovan to open a vault somewhere."

"Like obtaining a black book," I said. "Of clients' intimate information."

"Exactly," Karen went on. "Only there isn't one physically with Donovan Dynamics. He didn't keep a black book."

"So they wanted Nat," I said

"As leverage to get Mr. Donovan talking," Robert Frost chimed in.

My stomach churned with nervous anticipation, hearing about Nat.

If Nat had gone through any torture, anything like that, I couldn't bare hearing about it.

I looked over at Drew, and he had a stone face expression. I've only seen him once or twice before with that expression. Once when he was determined to win a race on the beach, and another time right after hearing about his mother Nadine Donovan's suicide attempt on

- 54 -

Fourth of July. I knew Drew was worried about Nat and his father, too.

I took a deep breath and prepared myself mentally and emotionally for any further news about Nat. *Oh God, please let Nat be alive and fine. And please let Mr. Donovan survive, too.*

In moments like these, you could taste your own mortality. You could feel everyone's own mortality.

Drew spoke up, commanding the room with his undeniable stage presence. "Have we located Nat and my father yet? Any progress on this?"

Joseph said, "I saw a light go off in the distance and another online. They seem to be heading across borders, but the good thing is…the signal is still on them, and it's moving. Which means…"

Drew said, "They are still alive." I saw him punch the air and bend over onto the table. When he stood up, there were tears in his eyes, and I went over to place my arms around him. Tim was there, patting Drew's shoulders too.

"It's okay, son," he said. "It's okay. We're all happy about the news and hopeful for something better."

Drew took a deep breath and contained himself. "How the hell are we going to get them out of there?"

"We have some inside help," Karen said. "Locals there. But we also have our own version of Special Forces. Men who used to be in Special Forces and Navy Seals."

"Other than the lights and some blurry images, poor audio, and satellite mapping, we can't get into the details without someone reporting back to us," Joseph said. "It's difficult at the moment to know what is exactly going on."

"When can we know for sure, and when can we get them out of there?" Drew asked.

"We're trying as hard as we can," Tim said. "Our teams there and here have been working thirteen hours straight or more these past few weeks. We are as dedicated towards finding Mr. Donovan and Nat as you are. Believe me, the survival of this company depends on it."

Drew looked at Tim and everyone else in the room and he stood up straighter. "Tim, Karen, Joseph, Kevin, and Robert, thank you for all your efforts and dedication. I appreciate it, and I'm sure if Nat or my father was here, they would be appreciative of your efforts, too. But we need to get them back here as soon as we can. If it takes another Special Forces to move in to get the job done, then we'll hire them. When it comes to the safety and lives of my father and brother, I'm not taking any chances."

The team looked at each other, and Drew crossed his arms, taking full control of the room. I could see the star quarterback in him rise at the moment, the charming natural leader whom guys liked to hang out with and girls wanted to go to bed with. I could see Nat in Drew...the resemblance strong as Drew looked more and more like a sexy young billionaire CEO in training.

"Let's get a second team of ex-Special Forces hired and dispatched today." He looked at his watch. "We don't have much time. The day is almost over. So, let's get to work."

Chapter 4

As tired as we were, we spent the rest of the day and night in that conference room with the team, working on getting another team of Special Forces assembled and ready to go. By the time Drew and I walked back to his car, it was almost time to get up for breakfast.

"Look Summer," Drew said. "I'm too tired to drive to my parents' house. There's a nice hotel nearby. How about we just go there?"

"Sure," I said. I wasn't in any mood to talk or do anything except sleep then.

"Good," Drew said, starting the car. We pulled out of the parking lot and within three minutes was pulling into the valet parking area of the Four Seasons.

"The Four Seasons?" I asked.

"Yup," Drew said. "The nearest nice hotel. I can't put you up in anything else. Plus, it was so close by." He grinned a tired grin and leaned over to give a quick peck on my cheeks. "We should rest while we're here, Summer. Take care of ourselves. Be good to ourselves. I know we're under a lot of stress, worries, and what not, so the best thing for that is to be kind to ourselves when we could. So here we are."

I couldn't help smiling at Drew and the sweet side of him that came out in the most unexpected but appropriate times. He was a gem, and spending time today with him only made me love him more.

"When did you plan this?" I asked.

"When I took a break between meetings," Drew said. "My mind's going in all different directions. It's like I have to keep going. I'm driven to see this through."

I nodded and then I remembered. Drew had made reservations sometime before in between meetings with the Donovan Dynamics team. Having no experience with special forces or global intelligence, I stepped back and watched the team worked. I was tired as dirt, but the energy in the room was electric, with Drew taking charge and moving things along, I could not believe this was the same Drew Donovan who was a manwhore player and don't-give-a-damn-about-the-Donovans-empire all this time. It was a complete transformation, and I have to say, it turned me on immensely. Drew was on fire, taking charge of Donovan Dynamics…a natural born leader in the boardroom as he was leading the football team. Why haven't I noticed that before? Why didn't I ever noticed things like that with Drew before…except only how he related to girls. Did all I cared about from Drew was his body and how I lusted over it? Was that the basis of my love or lust for him? He was so different from Nat, yet today, I saw how Nat and Drew could definitely be brothers. They both had that Donovan charm, that easy leadership and masculine strength. Even now, as bone-tired Drew must be, he was going a hundred miles per hour.

"Adrenaline?" I asked.

"That, plus, I know we have to do the right thing and bring them back quickly, whether or not that's the plan."

My head shot up then and a look of alarm went past Drew's face. "What do you mean whether or not that's in the plans?"

One of the valets came out and asked if we needed help with anything right then. "Nah, man," Drew said, looking relieved. "I got it." Drew walked to the car and grabbed my luggage, while hoisting his bag over one of his shoulders, carrying our luggage into the nice lobby. We were immediately checked-in as smooth as silk. No waiting, no need for an intensive inquisition.

"Mr. Donovan?" a pretty young girl with her black hair pulled back into a ponytail and wearing the hotel business suit came towards us.

Drew had his back towards her, but turned around as soon as he heard her name. "Yup, that's me," he said grinning his megawatt smile. The girl blushed and looked down slightly when she noticed Drew, but quickly recovered.

"Oh, you're so young," she said appreciatively. "Donovan Dynamics?"

"Yes," Drew said, straightening up. "Just came from there. Is there anything you need?"

"Oh," the girl said. Her name tag indicated her name as "Holly". "I thought you'd be older, being an executive there and all. You're very cute." She smiled, her green eyes focusing on his lips.

I wanted to smack her. Did she not see me? Did she realize how rude she was ignoring me as a person, but also ignoring me as Mr. Donovan's companion and possible girlfriend? The nerve of some people…

She turned her pretty head to take a good look at me before lifting her head up further and dismissing me. With a small smile and crinkling her green eyes excitedly, she said to Drew, "We have special rooms for our guests from Donovan Dynamics. I'll take you there, Mr. Donovan," she said licking her lips and visibly fixing her hair. She turned and walked in front of us, purposely swaying her hips a bit too much for someone who was supposed to just walk us to our room.

I watched Drew as his eyes fixed on Holly's butt walking seductively in front of us. Her strutting had its desired effects, and I wanted to jump in front of Drew, push Holly out of the way, smack her one, and turn around to smack him one. Just when I thought I'd do it, Drew slipped his arm around my waist, squeezed me, and leaned over to whisper in my ear. "Can't wait to get to our room, Summer. I know you're exhausted, but I can't wait to get you all alone with me, naked, and…" he stopped. "Whatever will happen between us, will."

I almost stopped walking as reality hit me in the face. Was I with Drew? Was I going to be with him? Nat is still alive so I shouldn't even think about being with Drew. All of a sudden, I felt sick. What was I doing? I went from missing Nat so much and being in such despair and grief over losing him…to sleeping with Drew and now about to share a room with him and probably ended up sleeping with him again. As much as I wanted him, as much as I was jealous with the flirting Holly was doing with him, I had to have some control.

I stopped. "Drew," I said, turning to him and stopping him. Holly was a few feet away and haven't noticed us not following her. "I need to get a room of my own."

"What?" Drew asked. "You don't have to do that. I can sleep on the sofa. Why? What did I do? Why don't you want to stay with me in the same room?" He searched my face earnestly. "What's the matter?"

"Drew, I do, but that's the thing…now that I know for certain that Nat is still alive, I can't be with you."

Drew looked like he wanted to punch something or someone. Then he took a deep breath. "It's not that…I want to be in the same room with you to watch over you. Be there for you."

"Can you honestly say you won't try anything if we share a room?" I asked.

Drew didn't answer for a while, but then he said, "Contrary to what you think of me, Summer, I'm not an animal. I have some control. If you don't want me to touch you or kiss you at all while we're sharing the room, I won't."

Secrets of the Fall (Donovan Brothers #2: Loving Summer #3)

I stared at him, at the sensual curve of his lips…lips that I couldn't seem to get enough of. "Promise?"

"Scout's honor that I won't push you to do anything you don't want, Summer. You're in control. I'll do whatever you say." He looked at me, his eyes softening. "I just want to make sure you're okay…that you'll be safe."

"Alright," I said. "We'll share a room."

"Good," Drew said as we began to catch up to Holly who had stopped in front of a set of double doors.

"Here we are?" Holly said, opening the doors and handing Drew the key. "The Presidential Suite."

My mouth fell open as I looked at Drew.

Holly walked in and opened the drapes a little more. The room was stunning with a hallway, an extra bedroom, a living room, and a balcony that looked out to the city. There were fresh flowers everywhere, including trays of fruit, breads, and cheese.

"If there is anything you need, Mr. Donovan," Holly smiled a seductive smile, "Just picked up the phone and it will go directly to me."

She gave me a hard look, lifted her chin, and left, closing the doors behind her.

I nudged Drew. "The Presidential Suite?"

"It's the only room they had under the Donovan Dynamics account. The rest of the rooms were booked."

"How? Is there some kind of convention for Donovan Dynamics?"

"No," Drew said. "No convention. Our operations and what we do are discreet. We didn't get too many rooms, and of the rooms we got, they were either the Presidential Suite or one of the other suites."

"That's nice," I said. "Donovan Dynamics is really doing well."

Drew shrugged. "I guess. I tried to stay out of it as much as I could…it was mostly Nat's thing, but Dad had me at the office once in a while when we were growing up. Even Rachel. We all know a few things about Donovan Dynamics. Not as much as Nat, though, but Rach and I aren't completely clueless."

"But the Presidential Suite at the Four Seasons?"

"Must be because I'm a Donovan," Drew said. "Plus," he took off my sweater and led me to the soft chenille sofa that felt heavenly when I sat down. "We need our rest. What better place to rest than here." He laid down on the sofa and indicated for me to lay my head on his chest.

"Drew…" I said. "You promised."

Secrets of the Fall (Donovan Brothers #2: Loving Summer #3)

"I promised not to kiss you or touch you if you didn't want it," Drew said earnestly. "But all I'm going to do is give you a massage." Drew looked innocently at me. "Do you want that at least?"

The idea of that sounded heavenly to me...being massaged by Drew's strong hands. His hands, used to gripping a football with such control and precision, always knew how to massage me when I needed it. After having sat in Drew's car for hours, then participated in meetings all night at Donovan Dynamics; I felt how stiff my back and neck was. I was beginning to get a headache too from lack of sleep.

"That's alright, Drew," I said. "You need to sleep...more than I do..."

"Hey, it's okay," Drew said. "My mind's too wired to go to sleep right now so I could massage you. It'll help me settle down. I need something to do with my hands." He smirked, "Besides working. I need to relax, too, and I can't think of a better way than to massage you."

"Drew...you promised," I said.

"I know," he said, turning me around and pulling me up on top of him so that my face was resting on his chest and he was kneading my back. Drew had always acted fast.

The next thing I knew, I was sound asleep on his chest, happily snoring away while his fingers twisted and pounded the stiffness out of my shoulders and neck. As attracted as I was to him, as much as I wanted to explore his body with my hands and lips, I felt comfortable and safe in Drew's arms, with his arms wrapped around me, holding me, massaging me. It was the first time since we've had sex that I didn't feel insta-lust with him, but a feeling of comfort and safety…the way I felt with Nat, whom I've always felt was my protector since we were kids and he stood up to bullies for me.

I drifted off into deep sleep, too exhausted to protest when Drew bent down and kissed me on my temples. It was chaste enough, and in a small way, I was a bit disappointed.

"Sweet dreams, my Princess," Drew whispered into my ear. "I will always protect you, always…even if I have to hide the truth to keep you safe. I love you more than life itself, but what I'm about to do…I hope you will forgive me when you understand why I did it."

Did I just dreamed Drew apologizing for something he was about to do?

Then I heard him talking to himself while I almost drifted off completely. "I made a promise that I've broken already today. I went against my promise, but it made you happy and hopeful, ready to live, ready to keep living. Oh God, why must it be this way? Why can't I tell you the truth? Why? I hate myself already for having to put her through this, but…if she only knew, she would understand. Dear Summer, please forgive me."

Chapter 5

Drew

I wanted to get Summer away from Donovan Dynamics as soon as the mission was accomplished. By "the mission" I meant the first meeting with the team in charge of Operations Rescue Family. It was close, having Summer at the headquarters all night long, while Tim and the team worked, securing a "Special Forces" team to rescue Nat and Dad.

It was a good thing everyone on that team have had specialized training and a background as ex-military, ex-CIA, and even ex-FBI. To tell you the truth, I was intimidated standing in the same room with some of these lethal and highly-trained, but seemingly harmless-looking Donovan Dynamics employees. But I had to keep up appearances, play a role, and act like I was taking charge, rather than following orders.

All for the sake of Summer.

That's why when she walked into the room, the Team was surprised to see her, shooting questioning looks at me that asked, "Why the hell did you bring her here, Donovan?"

I knew I should have just brought her here for a very short time just to say "hi" to everyone who worked on helping her with the cyber-bullying case before, but the entire finding another Special Forces team to rescue Nat and Dad seemed necessary to help Summer get through the day, to help her fight this grief of missing Nat.

While Summer slept on the sofa, I slipped out of the room and out onto the balcony. It was afternoon, not evening as it seemed, but we had just worked through the night without sleeping so was now facing the day. I touched a speed-dial button, and it connected me to a center.

"Input password," the voice said.

Kailin Gow

I inputted a password and then heard another voice. Deep, authoritative, and confident...the voice that ran Donovan Dynamics.

"Drew, son, I know why you concocted this plan with the second Special Forces team. It's a grand scheme, and I applaud you for thinking of it, but it is not in the plans. I know you want to protect her. I know you are willing to do anything to make her happy, but masking the operations with something like this will only jeopardize the true mission. Your brother and I had made this promise to Sookie before she died, and we intend to follow it through. If you continue with this scheme, with the intent to protect her, it would only hurt her more later. Nat is devastated by the possibility, but he's now accepted this is the way it must be. He would always love her, but Drew, this is the way it must be. Tell her now. Or let the team tell her. But it must be done quickly and swiftly while she has you to hold her together. Do it now, son, or the team will do it for you, and it will be harsher. In the next few days, our group will be heading into the heart of the operations. It is dangerous,

- 71 -

but this is where we are now. Why we are truly here. Summer would be proud if she knew, which she would one day. But for now...follow the plan."

I wanted to scream into the voice message how unfair and wrong it was to carry out what they wanted me to do. It wasn't as simple as that, especially if they could have seen how bad off Summer was after hearing about Nat missing. How she was so devastated she was going to take her own life. That was not like Summer. She must've hit bottom to even contemplate it, and I would do anything to keep her alive. Even lie.

I dialed into another number and spoke into my phone. "Thy will will be done, as it is in heaven and earth." Then I hung up. I spoke in code, using biblical references. No one could decipher it except those in the know. Somehow we were fortunate enough to still be able to reach and hear from Dad, through a special voicemail system Donovan Dynamics had set up so phone calls and voicemails could not be detected.

I walked back into the spacious and luxurious Presidential suite and laid down next to Summer on the sofa. I wanted to lift her up to carry her to the bed so she could sleep comfortably on there, but I didn't want to wake her. She was still in the same dress she wore when I first picked her up at the Pad to drive her up to San Francisco. A very feminine white cotton sundress with crochet lace. It was nicely fitted around the bodice to accentuate her tiny waist, flat stomach, and perky large breasts. It was the kind of dress that made guys like me want to tear it apart, want to be the hero, and want to be the gentleman to her lady. It was the kind of dress I loved seeing Summer wear because it brought out the tender loving side of me, the vulnerable side, and the side that just wanted to hold her, kiss her, and love her like a lady.

I watched her sleep peacefully against me, her breath gentle, soft, and warm near me, and her eyelids closed innocently like a baby's. I reached out to touch her soft long chestnut hair, bringing it to my nose as I smelled her jasmine-scented hair. She was so pretty I could stare at her the entire day. Just sit here and stare. I didn't need anything else from her. Just her presence made me feel good for being here. She made me feel good, like I was and could be a better man.

I wanted to punch the sky, but couldn't not with Summer on top of my chest. She won't think I'm a good person or have any potential to be good when she finds out about Nat and I.

Dad's message to me kept me from sleeping peacefully. I tossed and turned, trying to go to sleep, thinking what I had to do. By the time I finally fell asleep, it was dark. I was exhausted from the guilt, not so much from all the driving and the meeting. Physically, I could handle a lot. I had a lot of energy, which was why my sex drive was high, too. Why I went through girls like water when I was still in high school, before seeing Summer again. She was the reason why I became celibate. I haven't had sex with a girl since I told her I loved her and wanted to be with her. I just couldn't. I couldn't imagine being with anyone else but her. To me, that was commitment. I gave up everyone else for her, for the possibility to be with her. It may not seem that noble, but for someone who was a commitment phobe, mainly because I didn't want to be in a cheating relationship like the one my dad had with my mother, it was major. Now that bond between us was going to be tested.

Like I said, I finally fell into a deep sleep and began dreaming all kinds of dreams. I dreamt about moving to Malibu, moving into the Pad instead of the apartment I got to avoid seeing Summer with Nat. Then I dreamt of seeing Nat with Summer that one time I saw her in the showers, and afterwards seeing Nat raise her bra to lick her gorgeous tits. I was jealous seeing him with her, but at the same time, it was turning me on. I wanted to be the one licking her tits. I wanted to be the one sliding her black lace panties down her leg while I got down on my knees to lick her core. I shuddered, feeling how hard I've gotten just dreaming of me being with Summer.

But I couldn't stop. I was far too into my dreams, feeling harder and harder as I dreamt what could have happen if I had walked into the shower when Summer was showering, grabbed Summer from behind, and unapologetically pounded into her thrust after thrust with a few hip curls to get the most friction in her. It felt so good, holding her waist while she leaned against the shower walls, with me thrusting into her, with her moaning as I reach up and grabbed her breasts with both hands and teased her nipples to perfect peakness. I felt my hips sway and pound into her, my growls of pleasure mixed in with her moaning.

I kept thrusting until I exploded, and she climaxed. Sated, but not for long. She wanted more, and as I begin to touch her below to enter her again, she straddled me and took me deep within her. She took control of me, rode me until I was groaning. "Oh Summer," I groaned, "Fuck, you're good." I grabbed her butt and pressed her closer to me, while her breasts jutted out in front of my face. They were just the right height for me to latch onto one nipple, swirl my tongue on it for a bit until she was moaning.

"Oh Drew," Summer said. "I know we shouldn't, but this feels so good. And. I. Can't. Stop." She shifted her hips on me, while she rode me harder and faster. I was about to burst when something made me open my eyes from sleep.

My phone was ringing loud enough to wake Summer and I, but Summer was up already. And the sight she presented me when I opened my eyes was so beautiful, she could have given me a heart attack from shock. She was straddling me with her dress on…and moving back and forth on me, rubbing her naked wet core on my very hard hard-on. Not quite penetrating, but so close. As were her eyes…closed.

As though she was still sleeping and acting out her dream. Oh God, it was hot, especially since she had no inhibitions and if she could, she probably would be fucking my brains out with the speed and passion she was riding me.

She was a wild woman, moaning as she went up and down on me, her long hair flying everywhere. I was fully awake now, and enjoying Summer's sleepwalking so much I was reluctant to wake her up. It felt so good, I really wanted to enter her, but couldn't. This was strange for me…but I knew I had to stop her. Only I wanted to keep this going to help her build her sexual confidence.

Secrets of the Fall (Donovan Brothers #2: Loving Summer #3)

Being the gentleman that I was, I let her continue using my body for her pleasure. It wouldn't be fair to stop her right when she was needing me, or rather, my body the most.

I was relaxing, enjoying Summer take over and exert her sensuality over me. I loved it, and if she knew what she was doing, she would love it, too. Only thing was…did she know what she was doing?

"Summer…" I said softly. I had to wake her up now.

Her eyes were still closed, and she had bent down to start licking my chest and abs, lifting my shirt up so it was out of the way. But this felt so good…

"Summer," I reluctantly whispered.

"Oh, what?" she said in between kissing me and then taking my nipples into her mouth.

"It's time to wake up."

"Oh, silly, I am up," she giggled. She continued kissing down my torso then unbuttoned my jeans, unzipping it, and reaching into my underwear where her fingers began massaging me below. "Now, let's see how you taste, Nat," she said.

"Nat?" I yelled out of disappointment. Was she dreaming of doing all of this with Nat still?

My yell was loud enough to wake her up, startling her.

"What? What happened? Who yelled?" Summer asked, opening her eyes and blinking.

"It's okay," I said, touching her face gently. "You were just dreaming, and started to act out your dreams so I woke you up."

Summer blinked, completely oblivious to her dreams. "What kind of dreams was I having?"

"The same kind I was," I said raising my eyebrows.

Summer blushed. It was adorable how she could still feel so self-conscious about her sensuality with me, especially after all we've done. "Oh my goodness," she said. "What did I do?"

"You, um, kinda rode me, Summer," I said, smiling. "Not that I minded, but it was pretty intense, good, but intense where I didn't think you were sleep sexing."

"What?" Summer asked. "Sleep sexing…oh no, I don't even want to know what that means."

"It means what it sounds…you were acting out your sexual fantasies while sleeping…not that I mind."

Summer looked down and saw how she was sitting on top of me, straddling me, still with my jeans unbuttoned. "I am so embarrassed, Drew."

"Don't be," I said. "I highly enjoyed it. No complaints here."

"What did I do?" Summer asked.

"You were riding me and almost went down on me, but no, we didn't go all the way. I wouldn't let you if I knew it."

Summer blushed and looked down. "Oh Drew, this is so embarrassing. Why would I be doing that when I made you promise not to try anything?"

"I didn't try anything, Summer," I said with a smile. "You did." I took her hands in mine. "It was because deep down inside, you still want to."

Summer nodded. "I can't help myself, Drew. I do."

Chapter 6

<u>Summer</u>

After eating, showering separately, and getting ready to check out of the Four Seasons, we headed back to Drew's car.

"Where are we headed today?" I asked Drew, trying to act cheerful, despite knowing Nat was still missing. My heart didn't feel like lead though, as it did a few days ago. Nat was alive and still out there in dangerous territories. We had to get him back home safe as fast as possible. Like Drew, I was determined, even if I have to fly to wherever Nat was to help.

"We're going to drop by my parents' house to see how Mom's doing."

I didn't want to bring up how treatments were since Drew may be sensitive to it, knowing he might have inherited some of that mental disorder as his mother. Nat had warned me about it, but then he said he and Rachel could have inherited that mental disorder from their mother as well. The Donovan siblings all had that likelihood. Nat told me to keep an eye out on Drew and Rachel, as well as his mother.

As if he could read my mind, Drew said, "Since Nat left, I hired a live-in nurse to take care of Mom."

"That makes sense," I said. "Rachel's the only one living at the house at this point. Well, not really since she had gotten her school to accept internship hours for her working at Aunt Sookie's Acting Academy."

Drew visibly clenched his jaw. "Don't remind me that she moved to LA, and instead of staying with you at the Pad, she moved into live with Ryan, who is now living in his own apartment near East Los Angeles College. If my father and Nat were around, they would help me talk some sense into her, forbid her from seeing Ryan or at least moving in with the guy. Hell, she's my twin and the same age as me, but she sure seemed a lot younger."

"Rach is just rebelling again, like she did when she found out about your parents' divorce. Instead of living with your mother, she moved all the way to LA to finish her high school year with an internship teaching at Aunt Sookie's. I personally think Rach was smart for deciding that was what she wanted to pursue after high school. Like you and I, she wasted no time in pursuing her dreams. You went to USC earlier, and so did I. We can't blame Rach for wanting the same thing. Plus, as much as you and Rach love your mother, she needed someone with specialized training to help care for her. You can't put your lives on hold for her. Nat did in a way…" I thought about how he used that excuse to not allow himself to love me and to be with me, that he had too much family obligations to be in a romantic relationship with me for the longest time until he finally broke down and went for me.

Drew looked guilty then and licked his lips. "Nat sacrificed a lot for the sake of family," he said. "He was an incredible person and unbelievably amazing older brother."

I stared at Drew for a good second before I realized he said talking about Nat as though he was really gone. Where was the hope? Where was that enthusiastic drive to find Nat and bring him home alive?

"Drew...you're scaring me. Why are you talking about Nat that way?"

"Like what?" Drew asked.

"Like Nat was really gone," I said getting frustrated and even angry. "How could you refer to him like that, as though he was your brother. He would always be. What happened between now and yesterday when you were taking charge of organizing Donovan Dynamics' Operations Rescue team? We have a new Special Forces team sent out to find Nat and Mr. Donovan, find them and bring them home. That's something..."

Drew looked up into the sky and down again. He said, "Sorry, I was just tired. Didn't think about what or how I was saying things. Of course he would always be my big bro. Don't worry Summer, I'll take care of you and be there for you especially with Nat away..."

I took a deep breath and let out my frustration in one big breath. It was some yoga move Aunt Sookie had taught me years ago to help de-stress myself. I had started secretly or rather discreetly practicing yoga again in the mornings to help me deal with all of this…Nat, the stalker, the Academy, college, and Drew. Otherwise, I would be far worse than I could imagine.

I could also imagine what Drew was going through, having to take on all the responsibilities of Nat's, while still being expected to handle college, his football scholarship, his mother, Rachel, and me. I've been so selfish in my grief lately, not even realizing how all of this was affecting Drew or Rachel.

"It's okay, Drew," I said reaching out my hand to touch his shoulder. "I'm sorry. I shouldn't have snapped at you like that. I know you're tired and under a lot of stress, too. We will find Nat. We will get him home. I don't really know the details of the top secret mission he and your father was on, but I have hope." I reached out and hugged him tight, patting his back as I did so, in a supportive calming matter.

Drew sank into the hug, and reciprocated by holding me as tight against him as possible. I could feel his hard body pressed without an inch of space between us. "Oh, Summer," Drew let out a deep breath. "If you only knew how hard this is for me…"

"I know Drew," I said. "I'm going through the same thing. I know." I looked up into his face, my nose touching his, and my eyes looking deep into his. "You don't have to go through this alone. Just like I don't have to bear the burden of everything I have to deal with…with Aunt Sookie and now this. We have each other," I said looking so deep and earnestly into Drew's beautiful deep blue eyes. Our lips were so close, our face so close. I just wanted to give into the urge of kissing him, to help wipe out that hurt I saw through to the core of him.

I kissed his nose softly, playfully. "I see through you, Drew," I said. "You don't have to act big and strong around me. I know what you're going through too."

Drew inhaled deeply and then said through clenched teeth and a ragged breath, "No you don't, Summer."

I was stunned momentarily. Drew's never disagreed with me before. The one time I comforted him when he was going through his parents' divorce and his mother's attempted suicide, I was able to get through to him. We became closer from that experience. "No Drew, I do understand. You're trying to put a brave foot forward, to take the place of your dad and Nat for your family and for the company, but at the same time, you don't know if you will see them again, you don't know if your mother will get better or snap, you don't know if you could continue playing football when that really wasn't your passion to begin with, but your father's dream for you." I pulled his head to me until he and I were cheek to cheek. It's a gesture I did with him once when we were kids about seven or eight years old when we wanted to tell each other a secret.

"I'll tell you a secret, Drew," I said. "I'm scared too, but not so much anymore. I think when everything piled up all at once into a great big snowball, that was when it got to be too much for me to handle. I swear to God, Drew, when you found me in my bathtub, I must have hit bottom, lost my ground, fell, and kept falling, as though there was a black hole as big as the pit of nothingness. I wanted to go crawl into that hole to disappear, to escape the pain, but then I heard and saw you. I felt your love and your warmth. You did everything to made me feel you, even if you had to arouse me to get me there. But I did get pulled back from that pit. My body responded to your touch and to you, Drew. As yours respond to mine. Somehow or another we are connected, and even if we try to ignore it, we can't."

"Summer," Drew looked pained. "There's something I need to tell you, but first we have to go to see my mother. I have to see how she's doing. Then afterwards, I need to talk to you. Just remembered what you've just told me. How you are able to escape that bottomless pit of pain by connecting with someone by being there for someone else. Because I have a feeling we both will need it when I tell you the news."

Secrets of the Fall (Donovan Brothers #2: Loving Summer #3)

Immediately I felt a panic begin to rise within me, first from the pit of my stomach and on up through my chest and to my throat. *The news?* What did Drew mean by that? How could there be such dramatic news so early in the morning? What was going on?

"Drew, as much as I like surprises, I have a feeling I'll hate this one. Now I'm scared."

Drew pulled me into his arms and began rubbing my back, "No matter what, Summer, I've got you. I won't let you fall far. I've got you even if there is going to be something that you don't want to hear."

I felt tears beginning to form in my eyes. I hate feeling so weak and vulnerable. When did I get to become such an emotional basket case? When did I let myself break down like this?

"You're only human, Summer," Drew said. "We're only human. You're affected by good news, bad news, sad news, anything just like everyone else. It's what makes us sympathetic to others. It's what makes us capable of telling what's right from wrong. There is no shame in being scared or worried. I'm sorry, I shouldn't have said anything."

Drew turned away from me and hunkered down as though he was winded after running a few miles.

"Drew? What's the matter?" Now it was my turn to be concerned again.

Drew stood up straight and said, "Come on…let's get this over with."

I felt like my face was slapped. What's gotten into Drew to blow hot and cold like that? Was he displaying some kind of behavior related to his mother's mental illness?

"Drew," I asked calmly. "Are you alright?"

"I'm fine, Summer," he said, almost a little annoyed. He opened the door to the car, helped me in, and then buckled me in place. He was no-nonsense, serious even, as though his mind was elsewhere when he buckled me in, even without any emotions. Usually, he would linger when his fingers brush across my thighs, and I could see the pupils of his eyes dilate in excitement. But as he accidentally touched me, it was as though he had shut off all his emotions and was being a robot.

"Okay," I said, as Drew got into the driver's side, buckled up, and started the car. His face was grim as stepped hard on the gas pedal, careening us out of the parking lot and onto the highway. He was going faster than usual, as though he was taking his frustration out on the road. When we got to almost 90 miles per hour, driving pass every car on the highway, I said, "Slow down, Drew, we're not in a hurry."

"But we are," he said. "The sooner we get this over with, the better, then I could deal with the guilt."

I blinked. "The guilt? What are you talking about, Drew? There is nothing for you to feel guilty about. It's not your fault something happened to Nat and your father."

"No, it's not that," Drew said. "It's worse. It's much worse. But I can't tell you until I show you something."

"You can't tell me anything right now?" I said, crossing my arms.

"No, Summer, I can't," Drew said, setting his jaw.

"Okay," I said, feeling like a broken record with Drew.

Because of some miracle where there was hardly any traffic on our way from the Four Seasons to the Donovan mansion, we arrived in less than a half hour. The drive up the scenic hill would have been beautiful had it not been for how fast Drew was driving, making sharp turns, sudden stops, and fast jumpy spurts. By the time he pulled into the pavestone driveway, past the heavy iron gates to the garage, I was fuming.

He opened his door and got out, and was walking to my side of the car to open the door when I pushed it opened, got out and walked past him to the back seat to get my luggage. I didn't even want to make eye contact with him, I was so mad. How dare he tell me he had such ominous bad news, withheld it from me for a long time, making me suffer through intense worry and dread all that time, just to drive like a maniac to endanger our lives, and not even say a single thing the entire way over. How dare he ignore me the entire way over right after I spilled everything to him, right after I pushed aside my own worries to comfort him.

Secrets of the Fall (Donovan Brothers #2: Loving Summer #3)

How dare…

Drew took the luggage from my hands, dropped it down on the garage floor, closed the car door, and pushed me hard against it. Without a word, he grabbed my hair pulling it back while his mouth crushed into mine with a fury that melted me. I was burning just as much for him, as we passionately kissed each other, running our hands over each other, moaning and groaning our wants and needs.

His blue eyes pinned me down while he devoured my lips hungrily, my neck, and then my collarbone. He bit me on the fleshy part of my shoulders, and I felt a slight pain, but mostly pleasure as he licked it again, moaning. "Oh, Summer, last night was pure torture…you and your rules of not kissing or touching you." He probed his tongue into my mouth to taste my mouth, sending shudders of pleasure through me. He pressed his hips between my thighs, and I could feel how much he wanted me.

"You know," Drew whispered huskily against my cheeks as he pressed his hips harder against my hips. He took the corner of my mouth into his and sucked on it, making my lower body burn for him. "Rules get me more turned on, because they're meant to be broken. That's what I want from you. I want to break all your rules." His eyes burned into mine for a second before he released my mouth. He pushed my head back on the car until I was staring up into his face, his eyes still intensely on mine. "When you have no more rules in your rule book to break, Summer Jones, you will be mine."

His fingers came up to cup my chin to move my face to face his. He stuck a couple of his fingers into my mouth while his hips swayed and grinded against me. The pressure of him up against me, his hardness separated merely by a few pieces of cloth between us, sent a flame of lust clear through me and I bit down on his fingers in my mouth.

He groaned out of pain and out of pleasure. "Oh Summer, I didn't think you would have this wild side to you, but...it's refreshing." He removed his fingers from my mouth, his eyes never leaving mine. "All this time, I thought you were the good girl, of course you are," he grinned, "but you're more than that. You're a lioness waiting to break out of your bonds. You have all this sexy sensuality deep within you, hidden behind the prim and proper princess image you've portrayed all these years, but I know you Summer. I know how your body responds to mine, and there is..." he kissed me hungrily, "definitely more than the Summer Jones everyone knows."

I wanted to protest that he was wrong, that I was that prim and proper girl, but I knew deep in my heart, I was much more than that...that I had a fury in me that made me a survivor. I was not a delicate society girl, but a girl who could stand up to bullies, a girl who could run schools, a girl who led her volleyball team to the championships thus earning a scholarship to USC, a girl who was able to survive the devastating grief of losing her beloved aunt, a girl who was able to survive losing the love of her life, and now a girl who felt this fire that burned ferociously for a man whose passion matched hers.

Drew and I were both survivors with that passion within us pushing us pass the pain, the challenges, and anything that came our way.

Drew's eyes searched my face as he suddenly stopped and went still. "Do you understand what just happened?" Drew asked.

I nodded, my eyes wide and clear. There was no doubt I understood.

"You're a woman," Drew said. "No longer the girl you were when I visited you in Malibu last when Aunt Sookie was there. You've experienced so many things that could have broken you, but instead of breaking you, it made you stronger. It gave you this fire, this ferociousness, that drew me to you. I always wondered out of all the girls I knew, why I was so darn attracted to you, why I can't help falling in love with you. Why you…why not some other girl, whom my brother hasn't laid claim on. It's because I've fallen in love with this fire within you…the lioness within you, who had all the grace and loveliness of a dove. We can't help falling in love with whomever we do…I'm…" he smiled, suddenly looking a lot more like the carefree Drew I knew, "just so lucky to have fallen in love with you, Summer."

He kissed me gently and pulled back. The sweet Drew who spent the summer running with me on the beach, who took his time to woo me by cooking breakfast for me, by picking flowers for me, was back. It confused me with the sudden change in personality. He was a sexy and take charge lover a few minutes ago, which set me on fire, and then he became the sweet boy-next-door who reminded of Rachel's twin brother who would shyly hang out with Rachel and I while Nat went exploring on his own on the beach.

Nat had always been the natural leader of our group, mainly because he was older, but also because he had an independent streak. When I thought about him, he always appeared fearless to me, not afraid to go exploring, to take chances, nor try new things. I'd always looked up to him, since he was the eldest, and Aunt Sookie would often put Nat in charge of the twins and I when she needed extra help. Even at a young age, Nat was responsible, dutiful.

He never seemed like a kid to me. He was always as mature as an adult. He made me act more mature when I was with him…always treated me as his peer, the same age as him, rather than the same age as the twins.

Drew, on the other hand, had always been Drew…with his carefree manwhore ways, his lack of commitment to any deep relationships, his devil-may-care attitude. He had shown another side to him these past couple of days when we finally made love. It was as though he was waiting to reveal this part of himself to me…the serious side of Drew, the masculine and sophisticated side of him.

Drew took my hand in his and led me into the mansion. It was the second time I've been to the Donovan's castle-like mansion, complete with turrets, a circular driveway, heavy stonework, ornate iron gates, and marble everywhere. The Donovan Mansion was a stately masterpiece of architecture, which would make anyone proud to own, but when Nat first took me to visit, he said it felt like a prison. He felt suffocated at the family home, because he was far away from the place he loved – the beach at Malibu, and the person he loved – me.

No matter how luxurious or grand a house was, if you weren't with your loved one there, it still wouldn't feel like home.

"Summer," Drew said, leading me into the kitchen, the living room, the theater, and finally into a room I was familiar with...Nat's room. It was so Nat...from the straight no-nonsense lines, the dark heavy wood furniture and floors, the grey linen on the bed. Masculine chic. Nat had taste, yet it was down-to-earth and livable. "This is Nat's room. I'm sure when you last visited San Francisco with him, you've been here before." He looked at Nat's bed and visibly twitched his jaw. No doubt Drew had just pictured me lying on Nat's bed while Nat made love to me. Drew's seen it once or twice before by accident.

I looked at the bed, and I remembered Nat lying on top of me there, kissing me, and telling me how sorry he was for hurting me years ago by not keeping in touch with me, acknowledging me for years. The memory made me tear up, and I had to wipe away a few teardrops.

Drew went over to Nat's dresser where there was a photo of Drew, Nat, and Rachel together. Then there was a photo of Nat with me when I was thirteen and he was fourteen…the year the Donovans moved away to San Francisco, while I remained in Malibu, never seeing them again until three years later. Drew opened up the top drawer of the dresser and took out a small beautiful teakwood box. He handed it to me. "Open it, Summer."

"Is this from Nat?" I asked.

"No," Drew said. "It's Nat's. But I think you should see it."

I held the teakwood box gingerly in my hands, rubbing my thumb over the intricately-carved woodwork on the box. What was in this box that was so important for me to see? Without any more delays, I opened the box and looked down.

Nestled in the box amongst royal blue silk was a silver harmonica. I lifted it up and held it in my hand. Polished to perfection, the harmonica looked almost new, but upon closer inspection I could see it was an antique. Engraved on one side were the words, *Joseph A. Jones, 1912.*

I looked up to make eye contact with Drew. What did this mean?

"There's more," Drew said, taking out the blue silk lining. There was a small piece of paper folded inside. I pulled out the paper and gently unfolded it.

The handwriting was familiar as I read on…

Dear baby son,

I wanted to hand you something very special that belonged only to very special boys…boys who are descendants of Joseph A. Jones, a jazz musician extraordinaire, who pioneered music early in the nineteen-hundreds. You will one day be a pioneer, and I want to encourage you to reach out there, grab destiny, and hold on. I will miss being your mother, but you are in good hands. My best friend will be your mother, and she is married to a wonderful young man who will love and take good care of you as his own. Someday you will understand why I did what I had to do. I will always love you."

I will always be your mother,

Suzanne

I nearly tore the letter apart! That was Aunt Sookie's handwriting. What was a letter from Aunt Sookie doing there in the box?

Then it dawned on me...the reason why Nat would have that harmonica.

It couldn't be. No, it just couldn't be. I shook my head, hoping it couldn't be true...

One look at Drew's anguished grim face told me it was.

Nat was Aunt Sookie's son.

Chapter 7

Summer

I tore out of Nat's room as quick as I could, with Drew running behind me.

"Wait Summer, hold on," Drew yelled after me. I didn't want to hear anything more. I was in shock. Why didn't Aunt Sookie ever tell me she had a son? Why didn't Nat ever told me he was Aunt Sookie's real son? Suddenly everything made sense. The way Nat had almost the same coloring as Aunt Sookie. The way he acted differently than everyone in his family. The leadership trait and personality…very much like Aunt Sookie's.

Clues from the past suddenly made sense.

Kailin Gow

How Nadine Donovan, Drew and Nat's mother mentioned to me last time I visited her here at the mansion, that Aunt Sookie married the wrong man instead of the other one who was her perfect match. Aunt Sookie bore a baby once by that man, and her best friend Nadine, who was already married and stable, probably without the struggles a struggling actress like Aunt Sookie, had raising a baby on her own.

So Nadine adopted the baby as her own, while always sending the baby boy over to Aunt Sookie's for the summer to raise and spend time with his real mother. It was so shocking...I wanted to double check if that could be true. I needed to talk to my mother who was Aunt Sookie's older sister. I needed to confront her on this.

At the same time, I thought of what would happen between Nat and I. My heart sank. I didn't feel any perversion either. Only love. I still loved Nat, but now, if he was Aunt Sookie's son, then he and I would be blood-related. We would be too closely-related to even have children. A relationship between us would be taboo, forbidden.

Drew's arms caught me by the waist and he held me tight. "I'm so sorry, Summer. I didn't want to be the one to show you. But I had to let you know. I was shocked to find out, too. I mean, he's my brother still, but now I know we're not blood-related. That's why we're so different. But he's still a Donovan by adoption. I…"

"When did you know," I finally asked, wanting to understand. Did Nat know all along but didn't tell me, didn't let me know that we shouldn't, couldn't, be together?

Drew took a deep breath and said, "Nat didn't know until he was getting ready to go on the secret mission. Mom and Dad never told him he was adopted. Looked like they were going to take that to the grave if Nat didn't find this harmonica and the note. Even Mom was incredible in keeping the secret. Aunt Sookie's not here to ask and Mom denied it. Dad is gone…."

I had to sit down. My knees started buckling. We were headed downstairs, but I just sat down on the stairs and put my hand to my head. This was too much to take. It was as though fate had once again snatched Nat away, but this time, it was because we literally could not be together biologically. I felt sick to my stomach. Nat and I were blood relatives. And we had sex.

"Are you alright, Summer?" Drew asked sitting down on the stairs next to me.

"I'm just processing this, Drew," I said. "I'm in shock, but I'm trying to wrap my head around all this."

"Like I said," Drew said. "I hate to be the one to let you know, but there wasn't anyone else who could. Rach doesn't even know, and Mom is in denial, especially since she's missing Nat and Dad right now." Drew looked down. "You probably think I would bring this up so I can make you forget about Nat and choose me, but I couldn't do that, no matter how much I want to be with you."

"It doesn't matter," I finally said after a beat. "I still want Nat and your dad safely home. When Nat's back, we can deal with it together then."

A look of disappointment flickered across Drew's face for a very brief second, so brief I thought I had imagined it. "The team is working on it," he said. "Very hard. But, there are no guarantees no matter how much effort we put into it, no matter what we try. My dad and Nat knew the danger they were going to face going there, so it was their choice to go...well, actually my father's choice, but Nat went after him."

"Can we check in with the team at Donovan Dynamics to see how the search and rescue mission is going?" I asked.

"Yes, we will. But after we visit with my mother. She will be happy to see you, Summer."

"Of course, Drew, we have to see your mother," I agreed.

"Speaking of..." Drew stood up right when we heard the refrigerator door slammed. "I think she's back."

I stood up and walked down the stairs following Drew to the kitchen. As I turned into the kitchen, I bumped into a pretty auburn hair young woman carrying a bag of groceries into the kitchen.

"Oh, sorry," I said immediately. "Let me help you with that." I reached down to pick up an apple that had fallen to the ground, but Drew had already snatched all of them with his lightning fast football arms. He walked over to the girl, who was wearing a tight nurse's dress that hugged her curvaceous but fit body. He looked down at the girl, who was clearly blushing as she took him in with her blue eyes from head to toe. There was no denying she liked what she saw. This was Drew of course, and his charm was working on her like it did with others. "Here," he said, handing her the fruits one by one. I saw his fingers brushed hers when he handed her an orange, and she flinched, moving her hand back slightly. She was clearly affected, and Drew...Drew knew it, too. He smiled and held out his hand after the fruit was put away. "Hi," he said, "I'm Drew."

"I'm Amber," the girl said, "Amber Head, your mother's nurse." She stood up straight and said, "Nice to meet you. We talked on the phone before when you hired me, but now I'm real glad we finally got to meet in person."

Drew grinned, puffing out his chest. "Me, too!" He looked around and asked, "where is she?"

"Oh, Mrs. Donovan?" Amber said. "She said she was tired after spending the day at the country club playing tennis. She went upstairs to take a nap."

"How was she?" Drew asked. "Did she act strange or upset?"

"She acted fine considering what your family is going through," Amber said.

"No outbursts, no crying?"

"No, she seemed fine, and if she did feel upset, she took it out on the tennis game. She won a few rounds today," Amber smiled.

"I'm glad to hear that," Drew said. "If that's how she's been these past couple of days, then she's improved a whole lot."

"I think exercise and being able to meet some new friends at the club was good for her," Amber said happily.

Kailin Gow

I coughed suddenly, not on purpose, but because my throat was so dry. "Hi," I said walking up to Amber and extending my hand. "I'm Summer, family friend. Close family friend," I added.

"Oh, Summer," Amber smiled. "Yes, Drew's mentioned you a couple of times in our phone calls."

My eyebrows starting arching as I looked over at Drew. Phone calls...as in many phone calls regularly? They talk about me too?

I went to the refrigerator, opened the door, and helped myself to a water bottle inside. I grabbed another one for Drew and Amber and asked, "Want one?"

"Sure," Drew said, walking over to me and taking it out of my hands. Then he took the other one and handed it to Amber. His eyes never leaving hers.

My stomach started churning. What was going on? Was Drew flirting with the nurse Amber, or was this something more? They apparently talk on the phone a bit. She took care of Mrs. Donovan on a regular basis so he must call her all the time to check up with his mother.

The more I thought how close they quickly got without even having met until now, made me suddenly feel insecure. Did Drew actually liked Amber?

I felt like I had just been cheated on, although I had no right to claim Drew. It made me angry yet sad. Drew and I weren't together. We weren't even dating. What we did have was sometimes heavy lust-filled making out and one-time sex. Was that enough to sustain a lifetime?

Looking at Drew talking to Amber and completely oblivious to me; I wondered if I could even date date him without ever worrying about him straying. Women found him attractive all the time, plus he was friendly to everyone, the All-American hottie next door. He would constantly be tempted even if we were together.

Fed up with how he was openly flirting with Amber right in front of me, just after I learned about the devastating news about Nat; I was furious. What did I do to be treated like this?

"Drew," I said, walking up to him. "I'm going to go out to the car and wait for you. I take it, you've already shown what you wanted me to see."

I nodded at Amber and headed out the garage door to find Drew's car. I was ready to go. I was feeling weak, having to deal with finding out Nat was closer to me than I ever imagined. And now Drew actively flirting with his mother's new nurse.

Luckily the door was not locked. I threw open the passenger seat's door, played the radio, and sat in before the tears started.

Dammit, don't cry, Summer! I wiped away my tears and took out my phone.

SUMMER: Rach – can you get me on the Donovan private jet back to the Pad? Something's come up. In a hurry.

RACHEL: I can try. I just got authority to authorize an emergency. I'll get in touch with Steve, the pilot. Aren't you at Donovan Dynamics with Drew? Can't he get you on the jet?

SUMMER: Drew is getting it on with the girl taking care of your mom. Left me in the garage.

Secrets of the Fall (Donovan Brothers #2: Loving Summer #3)

RACEL: WTF is wrong with him? Listen Sum, I'll try to get the jet, but not sure how soon I can get you on.

SUMMER: Good because Drew is acting strange, and...

At that moment, the door from the house to the garage flung open, and Drew rushed out. His face apologetic and sad.

I got out of the car and stood by my door, my arms crossed. "If you think I'm going anywhere with you, Drew, think again. I'm heading home as soon as I can instead of spending..."

Drew tackled me to the car, plastering me against it, his hands roaming all over my body as his mouth crashed onto mine. It was a ferocity that was even more intense than the last time we were kissing here at the same spot. His hands reached underneath my shirt and bra, kneading my breasts before he tore open my front-buttoned bra and bent down to take each breasts in his mouth.

I was angry, in shock that he was once again blowing hot, but so turned on, I couldn't think. It was like his touch could instantly melt away all thoughts and feelings, except for this feeling of now. What he was doing to my body, to me, I couldn't ignore. The feelings and sensations were so intense, it pulled all my attention towards them. Like the time he made love to me…it brought me back from the bottomless pit of pain I was delving in before Drew's heated touch and lovemaking skills made me feel something else instead…something stronger. Lust. The basic animal instinct so strong and prevalent in humankind. Encouraged in men by their fathers to display it, but discouraged by society when it was found in equal measure in a woman. Drew had awaken my inner quest for sensual satisfaction, and he was my match when it came to the level of passion and drive we had for it.

If Aunt Sookie was still alive, I wouldn't know what she'd think of it. It was unbecoming for a good girl to be so sensual…to openly desire good and satisfying sex. Well, times have changed, and I felt Aunt Sookie would approve of the change. If she had Nat at another time, she probably would have raised him instead of giving him to the Donovans to raise. I cringed, thinking about Nat, my heart breaking to think I could never again kiss him or touch him or make love to him as we once did.

"Drew…" I said, as he kissed my stomach and made his way up. "I can't be with Nat anymore. We can't be together even if he comes back tonight or tomorrow. All these years I've been…"

"Hush," Drew said, taking my mouth with his. "You. Have. Me." He kissed me hard each time to emphasize those words. "And…I want it all. I want all of you, Summer." He pushed down my pants along with my panties, and shoved his fingers into me, making me jump nearly out of my skin with pleasure.

"Drew…oh my God, Drew," I moaned as he worked me to such heights, I felt my entire body give into the pleasure. "I'm going to…"

"Let it happen, baby," Drew coaxed. "Let go, just let go of all that tension, those feelings of anger, jealousy, pent up fucking desire." He unbuckled and unbutton his pants with one hand, and pulled it down. "All those emotions of anger, frustration, shock, jealousy, and even hate. Let me have it. I want them. Give them to me. Give me all that you have, and take it out on me now!" He entered me deeply, and I felt all of my frustrations and feelings as intense as they were before centered in on my lust for Drew. I moved with him, hard and as passionately as I could, taking it all out on him, driving both of us to the climax of pure pleasure and nothing else.

By the time the shudders between us stopped, we were sweaty and spent. I had my arms around Drew's neck, and he had his arms around my waist. We stared at each other for minutes drinking in each other as though we never wanted to break this connection, this touch between us.

"Gosh, Summer," Drew sighed. "That was the most mind-blowing experience I've ever had. Nothing compares to that." He shuddered just thinking about it. "I'm sorry about ignoring you like that earlier. I knew I shouldn't, but I wanted to get you riled up. I want to make you desire me with a passion as intense or more than your hatred for me at that moment. I have eyes only for you, Summer. No one else. Believe me, it was the hardest thing for me to act interested in a girl I have no ounce of interest in, when all I wanted was to grab you and make love to you all day."

"Had *me* fooled," I whispered, looking up at him.

"I know," Drew said. "I'm so sorry. But I really wanted to break through to you, make you act on how you feel instead of holding everything inside…all those feelings. Like Nat did. It's not healthy, Summer, to bottle all those feelings inside. It can make people do crazy things when they have too much pressure from that. I know, which was one reason why I was such a whore in school. It was a release. But you, you have no release like that, and with Nat gone, and you moving on…I want to be that release for you. I want you to use me, use my body for that, Summer. Because, Summer, you are definitely mine."

He kissed me long and hard until my toes were curling before pulling away and opening the door for me to get in.

I sat in my seat, and he reached over with the seat belt and sensually pulled it across me, brushing against my nipples and my thighs several times until they were sensitive to the touch. "Drew," I swatted his arm away after about the fifth time he readjusted the belt. "We have to get going." I laughed, and it felt good to laugh.

Drew smiled an innocent but wicked smile. "You totally get me, Summer," he said happily. Then he leaned into my ear to whisper. "You have me if you want me."

I felt a rush of heat soar through me and said huskily. "We really have to get going or we will have a repeat performance we don't have the time to do right now."

"Oh, Summer," Drew sighed, playfully. "You balance me. My total equal. What would I do without you?"

"Drive," I said. "Oh, I know what you could do without me, but it's more fun with me there." I smirked, and he laughed.

It was the first time in weeks we've been able to laugh. I thought I had forgotten how to, but now it was back.

Chapter 8

<u>Nat</u>

Sometimes to show love, to be loving, is to be able to walk away from that person you love. The hardest thing in life to this date is not dealing with my parents' divorce, my mother's mental illness, or college; it was walking away from love, from the woman I loved with all of my heart.

Again, it was the hardest thing I've ever done. I didn't think I would; I never thought that I could. But there were legitimate reasons why. And in the end when I made this decision to do what I did, I did it with the best intentions for her, for my family, for Drew, myself, and our country. It wasn't about me...and that was how I was able to walk away.

*****

I was dressed just like everyone else on the team…in camouflage so none of us stood out as we headed over to the headquarters. For weeks, they've prepped me on how to fight, how to use weapons, how to pass lie detector tests, and how to act if caught and tortured. For weeks, I've stayed in camps with these larger than life ex-marines, ex-army, purple-heart-decorated veterans and even heroes, who now worked privately as an army or Special Forces for hire. And for this mission, I had hired them through Donovan Dynamics. These men were part of my army. Being the youngest, the one without any military experience, and the smallest in build although I was as muscular and fit as any athlete; I stood out. I was the liability, but since I was the one with the intelligence and key information needed for this mission, I had to be trained to infiltrate just like one of them.

"Donovan," Tito Reed, a brawny tattooed ex-marine who stood 6 feet 5 inches of pure muscles including a head, bald, tough, and with a neck as thick as my torso; gestured for me to come up to join him in front. I moved my way up to the front, having been pushed back out of the way so the Special Forces could scope out the location while protecting me…the holder of the key.

"You see that?" Tito pointed, handing me his binocular. "That's the entrance we are entering through. There are two guards who rotate standing guard every four hours. They're small guys, but they're armed. If you get close enough to them in a fighting situation, the first thing you do is remove their weapon, then you have a fighting chance to take them down. If not," Tito handed me a large serated knife in a leather sheath. "Here are some back up." Then he reached into his leather vest, packed with weapons of all kinds. "You know what this is…" he took out a MK3 revolver. "We've practiced for weeks on this. You a damn fine shot now, too. It's yours. Take it."

I stared at the revolver before taking it and stuffing it into my own leather vest. The MK3 was the revolver of choice used by and specially made for the Special Forces, known as the SOCOM pistol, it was praise for its accuracy.

Having it on me, I felt like I was one of the guys now. I felt a little more secure knowing that if I had to protect myself, I at least had something to protect myself with…and gave me a good fighting chance to survive. I was going into this mission fully equipped and prepared. There was no cutting corners for this. If this mission failed, we would not be going home.

"Ok, Tito," I said. "I've studied the layout inside, know which room to search, and even know what to say if questioned. Are we ready to do this?"

Tito looked over at the other four guys in the group. They were silent but ready, each nodding their heads. "Ready," he said. "You stay behind me and Colby there. The other two, Hugh and Gao, come in from the rear."

"Gotcha," the men said.

Tito looked at me, and said, "Let's make this quick and painless. The faster we get in there and out, the safer it is for everyone."

My heart was beating so fast, and my hands were already beginning to sweat. I couldn't even answer back to

Tito because I was just hoping I could remember everything I was to do. My dad's life depended on it, as did a few other military personnel, whom he was working with before the operations went down. No one knew what I was doing, that I was here, that I was even alive. It was important for them to think that. Even my mother, Rachel, and Summer.

Summer…how I wish I could see her one last time, how I could tell her the truth. I would be lying if I said I didn't care what she would think about me lying to her, but for now, this was what I had to do. Sometimes you have to make choices that will hurt someone you care about deeply in order to help them in the long run. *Summer, if you know what I'm about to do, you would be proud of who I've become…for you. I've become a man who had to make those tough choices in life, for you.*

"Let's go!" Tito said, and like stealth ninjas, we moved as one unit hidden in the dark, blending into the background, through the forest and onto the heavily-guarded fortress.

Tito stepped to the side as we came up to the entrance, while Hugh distracted and took down the lone guard at the entrance. Quietly and efficiently. These guys meant business alright.

Tito led the way in the dark hallway in a maze of hallways, obviously designed to confuse and disorient intruders who weren't supposed to be there. Tito knew the way, and having prepped for this moment for weeks, I did, too.

We came to a section that split into three hallways, and Tito turned to go into the one closest to our right. I had to stop him, and point out that I thought it was the one straight ahead. He looked at me frowning for a second before he pulled out his tablet...a small one that fit into his large pocket on his vest. He nodded. I was right. He got in front of me and quickly led the way.

It was unusually quiet for what I imagined would be a busy headquarter for one of the largest cyber-crime rings in the world. That was how Donovan Dynamics got involved in the first place, hired on as an expert of security and cyber intelligence to aid the U.S. government and a couple of other countries who banded together globally to discretely find and dismantle cyber rings like these. It was such a top secret project, my father was personally involved in the operations.

It was so top secret, just a handful of executives at Donovan Dynamics knew about this contract. In fact, I was the only one who knew in detail what it was. Despite my age, I have already had years of experience being privy to Donovan Dynamics' operations and most confidential projects.

In fact, and this was another secret I withheld from Summer, because if she knew, it would put her in danger, she would look at me differently and not in a good way, and she would never forgive me for never contacting her or seeing her for those three years straight after we moved from Malibu to San Francisco.

When I turned thirteen, my world changed. Not only did I discovered how attracted I was to Summer as a girlfriend and had even gotten almost close to intimacy with her; but I got sucked into a world that was dangerous

Kailin Gow

and even criminal. I was a computer geek, nerd, genius-what-you-will; and had a knack for breaking through security walls and systems. I saw things that would blow anyone's minds. I saw the good and the ugly. Unfortunately mostly the ugly since people tend to use the computer and the internet for anonymous things they were too ashamed to do in public.

I got into the world of hackers, saw that they were able to infiltrate into people's personal computers, able to point people's own webcams at themselves while the hackers laughed and made fun of the people they labeled, their "slaves" or "minions". It was like the Sims Game to the hackers, being able to manipulate people by playing with them.

It was an ugly subculture, which I was ashamed to have fallen into when I was a young teenager. I didn't have any friends, had moved to a new city with a new school, and all this pressure to succeed. I was like these boys who wasted hours playing these hacking games. That was why I was too ashamed of telling Summer why I didn't see or try to keep in touch with her right after my family moved. It wasn't her at all. It was because I did some stupid things, got involved in some stupid idiotic groups, and was too ashamed of it all. Summer was pristine, good, pure...she would not look at me again if she knew.

But my dad knew, and it turned out, it was the kind of talent he needed to help grow Donovan Dynamics into a worldwide security firm. The cyber-security and intelligence division of it grew in leaps and bounds because Dad had put me in charge. At thirteen years old, being a former hacker, I was already running a major division in a fast-growing company.

But no one knew this, except for Dad and myself...and maybe Drew, who suspected I had more to do with Dad's company than just some kind of internship. It was inconceivable and even somewhat illegal that I would be doing all of these hacking activities in the line of work. Although it was for good intentions and good reasons, hacking for Donovan Dynamics, was still hacking. Illegally or legally, it was still, to me, an invasion of privacy.

But as much as I was ashamed of it, I was proud to be able to use my talent toward helping solve cyber-crimes for corporations, for the government, and respectable organizations. Using my talents, I was also able to keep tabs on Summer when she was younger. After we moved to San Francisco, I couldn't help it, but I hacked into her computer once or twice, just so I could see her face when she looked at her screen. It was a way for me to keep in touch with her (although she never knew). Like I said, it was wrong, and I felt horrible for even trying. Soon after hacking twice into her computer, I stopped.

I even tried to stop working for Dad. But he needed me, and eventually, he ended up hiring more people, and I was able to slowly pull away from Donovan Dynamics while getting more into school, football, and making friends.

But here we are now…in the middle of enemy territory, smack in the center of cyber-crimes central. With me getting ready to do the biggest hacking or computer infiltration I've ever done…with so much riding on it.

The Ex-Special Forces team and I continued down the hallway into an area that looked a break room with tables, a small kitchen, some sofa. Who knew organized cyber-criminals had a need for a breakroom and coffee, too.

We went pass a large room that had a window from the outside of the hallway looking in. The room was dark, but I could see the outline of old-fashioned desktop computer monitors on top of the rectangular tables lining the room. It looked like it could fill up to hundreds of people at a time, working on the computers. It was evening, and the workers had gone home.

I gestured to Tito about going in, but he stopped me and pointed to another room tucked away in the back of the main computer mill room. He pointed to that room.

The team made its way into the room, half of us inside, while the other half outside, as Tito led the way into the office. It looked like any typical office of any corporate building. There was a desk, a computer, stuff on the wall... I immediately put on my gloves, went to the computer, which was left on, and quickly got through the security

Kailin Gow

wall. Next I went into the files, searching for the one that held information that was vital to international security.

It was under some obscure name, but I found it, and went deep enough to obtain what I needed.

I turned to Tito with a thumbs up, and was about to erase all tracks and put the computer to sleep when I noticed a small red light on the computer turn on with a click. Shit, it was the monitor. I gestured for everyone to get out of the view of the computer monitor, ducking down myself so I was completely out of the view.

Being the ex-hacker that I was, I knew a hacker had gone into that computer, turned on the camera, and was checking out the room.

Smart. These cyber-criminals knew how to keep their information safe and how to secure themselves. They didn't need heavily-armed guards standing watch everywhere. All they needed were monitors in each room, capable of checking on everything.

After about five excruciating minutes of the monitor being on, the red light went off. I finished everything up, and stood up, along with the other men.

Tito stepped outside first with me following and the rest. It looked like a smooth, quick mission with no hassles as we neared the exit. But that was short-lived. One of the monitors near the exit turned on, and caught us about to storm the door leading outside.

We opened the door. Tito knocked out the guard standing next to the door, and Gao broke the neck of another guard who saw what happened and had ran up. Hugh stopped another guard as Tito grabbed me and pushed me forward with him towards the fence. "Run and don't stop!" he yelled, shoving me through the fence while trying to follow me through.

I looked back, and saw that Tito was too big to go through the fence and had taken off his vest and weapons. He was half way through when one of the guards grabbed him from behind. Tito turned back and punched him in the face so hard the guard's nose broke and blood spilled everywhere as he fell backwards.

Tito saw me standing there, and he barked, "Follow the plan. Go!"

I wanted to go back to help Tito through the fence, but he was right, now that the cyber-criminals know about us, they could very easily go in and change everything in their system, rendering everything I've just accomplished, useless.

I only had a few minutes to get to the next step or everything, including, and I'm hoping it was not the case, giving up the Special Force's lives for this mission would be in vain.

Chapter 9

Nat

It took me less than five minutes to weave my way to the van hidden in the forest and covered up by bushes as camouflage. The van had served for our headquarters for the past week, and held our computer equipment, satellite, and everything we needed. I opened the door, jumped in, and went straight to the computer, typing as fast as I can through the security and then to another hidden wall.

It was the special private space set up for Donovan Dynamics Elite. I typed in the information I saw at the criminal headquarter, downloaded it, and immediately got an answer.

"Well done," the message said. *"Now let's go home."*

It was from John. John was code for my Dad when he was in the field.

"Will this get her out? Will it get you out?" I typed back.

"The key is opening the vault. It was the right code. You did it. Amazing work, son."

I breathe a deep sigh of relief, while starting the van. As much as I wanted to stay around to help out the guys, I also knew that if caught by the ruthless criminal of that operations, with this van full of sensitive information and equipment, it would be far worse. I had to make the decision to leave. Tito had barked the order for me to "Follow Plan".

The Plan was simple. Get the job done. Get the hell out. That was the Plan.

Secrets of the Fall (Donovan Brothers #2: Loving Summer #3)

So I was getting the hell out. Driving out of the forest and onto the road as fast as I could. Too much was riding on me completing this mission without my emotions getting in the way. I felt horrible, devastated even for leaving Tito and the men behind, but they were professionals. They knew the danger and what was the priority. They also knew how to get the hell out if they needed to. I felt bad for them, but I also had the utmost confidence in them.

I dialed my phone to the hidden voicemail system that Donovan Dynamics used for the field. "Left 5 men at CS2 location. Send backup or at least transportation to pick them up."

I pray to God, this wasn't in vain. At least I knew the vault had opened, because of the code I found on the computer back at CS2. That meant my father had fulfilled his obligations to those who were holding him, meaning he was going to be let go, along with another very important person in my life: Major Jones, Summer's mother.

*****

Just when I thought my father was a complete a-hole for cheating on Mom with his secretary, I discover another side to him that made me withhold judgment. Dad had taken on this dangerous contract for Donovan Dynamics because he got word from Aunt Sookie the last week before she died about how worried she was for Summer's mother going on a super secret mission which she didn't know when she would be returning. That was why Aunt Sookie had Summer move into the Pad permanently that summer. Aunt Sookie had gotten my father to promise he'd use Donovan Dynamics' influence to help keep track of Major Jones, and if something happened, to step in.

It turned out shortly after Major Jones left to go back to work, to the mission straight from seeing Mom in San Francisco after Mom had her suicide incidence; she went missing. There was far too much bureaucratic work to even get a search team looking for Major Jones, so we took this under our own hands, privately and quickly. Summer didn't even know her mother was missing. With everything she had to deal with following Aunt Sookie's death, telling her would only cause her more worry and grief. No, my father and his team was going to go in, locate Major Jones, and bring her home safely even before someone from her division would lift a finger to start the paperwork to get a search team out to bring her home.

Because her mother was involved in this and was in a life and death situation, the utmost discretion was necessary. I couldn't let Summer know anything. I couldn't let Drew know. Nor Rachel or Mother. Not letting her know was for her own good. Also, me disappearing for this mission was necessary. I knew it would cause her pain and grief thinking I was missing, but then again, it was necessary for me to accomplish this mission. What was more important…her mother being found and alive or me lying to Summer about me being alive and well? It wasn't even a lie, it was a circumstance, an impossible one, which I was bound from revealing.

I checked into the voicemail and found a new message. From John.

JOHN: They got what they wanted and released Major Jones Will be releasing me when they get the second vault opening. Taking some time.

BTW Drew followed the plan. Summer was informed.

My heart sank. Summer knew now about my other secret...one I just found out myself...that there was a possibility I was closer to Summer than we both could imagine. It was a shocking revelation for me to find out that I could be Aunt Sookie's son. That I could be closely related by blood to Summer. Mom never confirmed it, and Aunt Sookie never mentioned it, even on deathbed.

Dad, well, he said there was a possibility. When Dad and Mom first married, they couldn't have a child for a while. They were desperate and looked into adoption agencies. They were young, too, and barely starting out in their careers. Well, one day Dad heard from Mom that she had a baby boy to adopt from a mother who was single and didn't have the means to raise the baby. Mom knew the mother very well and could vouch for the health of the mother. When they saw the baby, they fell in love with the baby boy, and didn't care who gave birth to him as long as he was theirs. So, Dad never did cared or realized who my real mother was. Until now…if there was a possibility that Summer and I were blood relatives, then for sure, we could not be together.

I didn't know until the night before I took off for the mission and found a harmonica from someone named Suzanne to me. My father had kept it for a while along with some of his most valued possessions. I wouldn't have found it if I had not been searching for one of the codes, which only Dad had, but had given me access to, too.

Of course I was devastated when I thought of the possibilities. Could I still have a future with Summer if we were related? I don't know. I was such a stickler to tradition and doing what was right…by society's rule. If she was my first cousin, could we get married? Could we have children?

All I wanted to do was to answer "yes" to all of these questions. To screw society's expectations and norms. I loved this woman to death, and I want her entirely including sexually. I didn't want something like our love becoming some kind of perversion.

Yet, deep down inside, I knew it was the right thing for her to know...even if there was a possibility...so she could decide whether being together would be worth the scorn, worth risking everything for, worth the taboo or for her to move on, maybe find another love without those extra challenges.

To move onto Drew, whom I knew deep within me, Summer also loved. The heat between them was undeniable, and if she chose him rather than me, I knew for certain, I could not bear to see them together, at least for a while. Yet if she chose me, there were going to be challenges for us. Biologically, we may not be able to have children together, which if she does choose me, I know I would like to consider with her.

So Drew had told her. I wonder how that made him feel. Was he able to tell her without gloating to her about it, and then quickly stepping in to replace me? I was jealous just thinking about Drew and Summer being together. If they were together, I'd move far away from them, live on some kind of remote island so I wouldn't even have the possibility of bumping into them.

I heard a buzzing and turned to my phone. A message had come in through the remote voicemail I had just set up.

JOHN: I am free. Walking to meet Major Jones at the nearest location where they have taxis. See you soon at our hangar.

My heart lifted, and I let out a deep sigh of relief. "Thank God!" I yelled punching the air. I almost had tears in my eyes, I was so happy and emotional. A whole wall of worry lifted from my shoulders, and for the first time in weeks, I was able to really smile.

Chapter 10

<u>Summer</u>

Drew and I were called in for an emergency meeting at Donovan Dynamics shortly after we left the Donovan Mansion. From the look on Drew's face, he didn't know what it was about, either. Whatever it was, I was trying to prepare myself. Sometimes mentally preparing for some news could help with stressful news, but I knew whatever the news was going to be, I would be deeply affected.

I loved Drew with a passion, loved being with Drew physically like the way we were, but I still loved Nat, no matter what we were. Again, there was no closure. So, heading back to Donovan Dynamics was the closure I sought. I had a feeling deep down inside that there would be breakthrough news. We have all been hoping. We have all been praying.

Rachel was even going to meet us there. She had decided to take the company's private jet to fly here for this meeting, and if I was having any problems with Drew, as I had text her earlier about, she would fly back home with me, while Drew could drive back on his own.

While we were driving, I glanced over at Drew, who was gripping the steering wheel so tight, his knuckles were white. "Hey Drew," I said. "You okay?"

Drew's head jerk up for a second, startled, as he said, "What? Oh, nothing wrong. Just thinking."

"More like worrying," I said. "What are you worried about. Share, Drew. You told me to open up to you a while ago, now you could do the same with me."

"Okay, Summer," Drew said. "I did, and I should." He smiled at me, reaching out his hand to cup my cheek while thumbing my lower lips, rubbing them until they were swollen, as though they were bruised from hard kissing. "Gosh, Summer, I know we just fucked as long and hard as possible, but I'm getting hard just sitting here touching your lips." He stuck his thumb into my mouth, and I instinctively wrapped my lips around it, sucking on it, while he closed his eyes in pleasure slowly and then opened them. "Oh, that about made me pull over by the highway, Summer."

As much as I was trying to stay focus about going to Donovan Dynamics, I was just as aroused. "Why don't you?" I asked.

Drew gave me a pointed look before he raised his eyebrows. "Are you asking me to?"

"I'm saying, if you need to check out something, for the sake of safe driving, maybe you should." I said innocently.

"Well then, that makes sense. For the sake of driving safely and getting my mind out of my dick, I'm pulling over to check something of yours out." He pulled over into a remote area off the country road. Somehow he took the long route to Donovan Dynamics from the Donovan Mansion...one that involved country roads, private fields, and hidden hills.

As soon as the car parked, Drew unbuckled me and pulled me on top of his lap, where he had unzipped his jeans. He pushed my pants and panties off, and nestled me right on top of him. With a swift thrust, he entered me, and I was writhing on him, riding him, while he pushed aside my shirt and bra to suck on my breasts. We kept riding and thrusting until we both climaxed. Afterwards, Drew cupped my face and pulled me up close to gently kissed my lips. "I think after that, Summer, you are officially mine."

He was staring at me so intensely with such confidence and determination, I almost wanted to agree with him. But I just couldn't. Not until I have closure.

As though he could read my mind, Drew sat back down, pulled my shirt and bra back down, and fixed my pants before lifting me to place me back in my seat. He was silent the entire drive to Donovan Dynamics.

I was still high on my Drewgasm but a bit awkward with the silence between us. I know he wanted me to say "yes" and commit only to him now, but I just couldn't until I knew what happened to Nat and where he was.

The awkward silence was happily broken when I spotted a familiar figure bounced into our view.

Rachel Donovan was wearing her signature Rach look with a plaid skirt, purple tights, black patent lace-up boots, and a black bustier satin top under a black leather jacket. Her hair was still straight black with a streak of purple chunk around her face. She was bouncing up and down in excitement as she ran over to my side of the car, trying to open it.

"Hey, Sum!" she squealed. "My gosh you look great! Love that wild bedroom hair. So sexy, Sum!"

"Hi Rach," I squeezed her, hugging her so tightly. I love my best girlfriend Rachel like no other. Although she was Drew's fraternal twin, she was not like him at all. Cute, bubbly, and downright bold. "Did you just get here?"

"No, been here for half an hour so I couldn't wait to see you two. So awkward sitting there in the boardroom by myself with all the suits, you know."

"Dad's team," Drew corrected. "'Technically our team."

"Suits," Rachel said. "They were all wearing suits. You know how uncomfortable I am in that kind of environment. It's like being in the Principal's Office, you know."

Drew shot me a look and rolled his eyes. "They are our staff, Rachel. They're helping us find Dad and Nat. They're the ones we're relying on to get them back home. Be nice."

Rachel looked offended. "I am nice," she said. "I'm always nice." She looked at me, "When have I not been nice?"

"Well when you dumped your milkshake over one of the mean gossip girl's heads at the nail salon," I recounted. "When you concocted a grand and masterful publicity stunt for Astor's breakup with me…"

Rachel was indignant. "Those girls were talking crap about you without even knowing you. When someone is mean to you for the sake of just being mean and hateful, you have a right to stand up to them. Dish out their own medicine. Put them in their place. Mean people should face the music. Treat those as you would have them treat you. So if they're mean they should get treated meanly by others, too."

"I don't think 'meanly' is a word, Rach," Drew said.

"Can't I make up a word when I feel like it?" Rachel said. "If I can't find a word to describe something, can't I make up a word for it. It's a free country. I'm free to do what I want."

"Oh brother," Drew said, lifting his hands and shifting his feet. "And we're going to be taking over this massively successful very professional, highly trustworthy organization our father built one day? Rachel," Drew grew a little serious. "We're not in high school or middle school anymore. Your attitude and manners are still pretty immature. How are you going to stand up and talk numbers and security to CEOs of multinational corporations, to top politicians around the world, to agents and managers of celebrities who employ us? Rachel, Summer and I had to grow up overnight to deal with the details on finding Nat and Dad. We had to sit through logistics, plans, and stuff that are crucial in helping us accomplish this. There are no room for childish complaints right now. I know you want to deny everything, that it doesn't exist because you've shoved it under the rug, but it's there, and we have to deal with it as mature and grown up as possible."

I was stunned, and Rachel just stood there speechless, her mouth hanging open in shock.

Then her blue eyes squinted close, opening them again to reveal unshed tears. "How dare you, Drew! How dare you question my love and loyalty to Nat and Dad. Just because I'm not in that stuffy boardroom poring over plans like you and Summer doesn't mean I don't care. I do. I want them back as badly as you. I missed them, too. But I guess you haven't noticed. I'm not in your group of two to share in the comforting and the supporting. You two have each other. You two understand what it's like to go through all this, but I have no one. It's just me. Ryan's not even my boyfriend. He hasn't been for months. He's there as a good casual lay, but other than that, he's shallow, and he doesn't understand us. Doesn't care to understand our crazy family. We broke up a while back, but get together just to hook up."

Rachel broke down crying, and I went over to hug her tightly. "I'm so sorry, Rachel. I should have been there for you. I've just been so preoccupied in my own grief, I haven't noticed anything else. I'm sorry about Ryan, too."

"It's okay," Rachel said. "I'm glad I broke up with Ryan. Besides our style of dressing and music, we didn't have anything else in common. He wants to work on cars and one day manage his father's garage. I have zero interest in that. Plus I'm young, and I want to act. I love kids. I love teaching at the Academy."

I smiled. "I'm glad you are there, Rachel. You are a lifesaver for taking on a lot of the Academy management duties. It's true...although you're not here doing the logistics planning and stuff like that for Donovan Dynamics, you're helping out by helping take care of things at home. I am so so sorry for not being there to help right now. I can't believe how dumb and thoughtless I was…how low I've sunk into despair and depression over this whole thing that I've abandoned my best friend in the world."

Rachel loudly blew her nose on a tissue she found in my purse, which she'd opened to look for one. "It's okay. At least I got to hang out with Astor a bit at the Academy whenever he could make it in. He really loves the place, and has his heart in the right place. He wants to keep Aunt Sookie's legacy alive, and I think he's the coolest person for doing all that."

I smiled. Oh Astor, how I miss my first so-called boyfriend, who happened to be a celebrity actor. "He's amazing, isn't he?"

Rachel smiled widely. "Yes, he is. After teaching a class with me, he even offers to buy me ice cream down the street from the Academy. It's so easy to talk to him, Sum. He's more down-to-earth than anyone imagines. He's funny, too…does a mean impression of Lady GaGa." Rachel bent her knees and started shaking her booty back and forth, her arms raised in the air." I laughed.

Drew even laughed.

"He does the entire get up, too. Arrives in a space alien costume or a large sandwich," Rachel went on. "The kids love it."

I could imagine Astor doing that on stage. "I bet."

Astor was an incredible actor, boyfriend, and student. He was Aunt Sookie's star student, and I met him through her school. I sighed. I still had such an affection for him. I couldn't help myself. He was charm personified. But between his crazy fans, the long distance relationship, his jealous starlet co-stars, and my own complicated relationship issues, it was too hard for us to stay together. I loved him but my connection with the Donovan brothers was so much deeper. Between having a lifelong crush on Nat to finally noticing Drew who had a lifelong crush on me, my love life was too complicated as it was. To have Astor even be part of that...

Rachel was fixing Drew's hair. Not that he needed it, but she was fussing with it. "You should wear your hair this way, Drew, like Astor. Astor has the hottest hair. It has body, it's shiny, and it very grabbable."

"Rach!" I laughed. "Oh my God. You do not have a crush on Astor."

Rachel turned around so quickly to look at me, I thought she'd have whiplash. "What do you mean, Sum?"

"The way you're talking about him," I said. "You are gushing."

"I am not," she denied, turning pink.

"You are," Drew got into it. "Rachel, it is obvious. I bet he could even tell, but he's too much of a gentleman to tell you to back off."

"Nice, Drew," Rachel said. "That's a nice way to talk to your sister. If you can't say anything nice about someone, then don't even open your damn mouth."

"Alright alright," Drew raised his hands in surrender. "I'm just messing with you. I'm happy you found a guy who could stand being in the same room with you for even five minutes…"

Rachel shot daggers at Drew. "Really? Is that the best you could come up with?"

"Don't even get me started," Drew said.

Kailin Gow

"Um, talking about getting started you two, we need to go into the boardroom. I bet they're waiting for us, and here we are throwing insults at one another," I said, straightening my pants and shirt. I checked my make-up and hair, making sure I looked presentable. Drew was right. When you enter a professional organization, you have to be professional, especially when we were supposed to represent the founder and CEO, Mr. Donovan.

Drew came around to me and put his arm around my shoulders. "Come on, Summer," he said. "You're right. We don't need to add to the suspense already." He looked at me with the most sincere eyes. "Maybe this is closure." He put his other arm around Rachel's shoulders and led both of us inside the Donovan Dynamics building.

Nothing's changed since the last time I was here with Drew except Rachel was here. As much as I loved Drew, having Rachel here made me feel much better. We were a family, no matter what. As we made our way up to the executive meeting rooms, that bond we had felt stronger and stronger. All this…all the people working at Donovan

Dynamics were hoping for the same thing…that Mr. Donovan and Nat would be safely arriving home soon.

We walked into the Executive Boardroom where Timothy and Karen, along with the other international security team members were waiting.

"Hi Drew, Summer, and Rachel," Timothy said, standing up to shake our hands. "Glad you could make it in on such short notice. Since everyone's met before, no need for introductions so please have a seat."

I greeted everyone and then sat down between Rachel and Drew at the large oval table. I looked at the faces of everyone and tried to decipher their expression. Did they know the news already? Was it good news or bad news?

Timothy came up to us and instead of standing in front of the room as though he was going to conduct a meeting, he came and sat down with us. "Look, I know we're at a corporate boardroom and all, but this is more of a family matter than anything. I have children close to your age, and I can imagine what you are all going through having your father and brother missing. You don't have to put on any professional or corporate image with us. We may be a billion dollar corporation, but we're a family business too. I've known your father from day one of him starting this corporation, and have known him even before. He and I were in the same unit. We're friends and not just colleagues. So I have a personal stake at helping with this operations, too."

Timothy looked around the room and said, "We have been briefed with what the situation is. There's good news and not so good news." Timothy looked at Drew for a brief moment, and I thought it was because Drew was the Donovan put in charge of the rescue mission. I saw Drew looked down, his hands shaking. Whatever Drew knew, I was getting worried. Did Drew know more than he seemed?

Rachel, who had never been one to refrain from saying whatever was on her mind blurted out, "What happened? What freakin' happened to my brother and father, dammit?"

Timothy said, "The good news is, your father was released from where he was held hostage. He is alive and well. There was another person from military released with him, and she was in good health."

"So they're coming back home?" Rachel asked. "Dad and Nat?"

Timothy said, "Mr. Donovan is heading back today, along with the other hostage. Unfortunately, Nat's whereabouts are still unknown."

Timothy's face literally looked more wrinkly and tired, exhausted even as he looked over at the members of his team. He was about to say something when Drew asked, "What about the Special Forces? Were they able to locate him?"

Timothy's eyes blew up wide as he stared unbelievably at Drew. He said, "It was not in the Plan, Drew. You knew that."

"But we went through all the motions to set up a Special Forces," Drew said.

"You did," Karen joined Timothy. "You wanted it to seem as though we did get a Special Forces team, a second one to go in."

"Didn't you?" Drew asked. "It could be done..."

"Didn't you get the message, Drew? It was not in the Plan."

Drew got and looked at Karen and Timothy. "Let's make it in the Plan. This time it is."

"Why?" Timothy asked. "We thought that would be the best way."

Drew looked over at me, sitting there, not quite sure what was happening except that Nat was still missing. Gosh, Nat was still missing, yet Mr. Donovan and some military person was flying back tonight. I spoke up. "Tim, Karen, everyone...Nat is an important member of Donovan Dynamics and a very beloved member of this family. Is there anything we could do to find him? Anything else? It doesn't make sense that he was out there to help save Mr. Donovan, had gotten Mr. Donovan released, but now went completely off radar. Someone has got to know what happened to Nat."

"We'll try out best," Timothy said finally. "If we have to send another Special Forces team, we will."

"Good," Drew said. "We have to at least try." He came over to me and put his arm around my shoulders. "We'll find him, Summer. Don't worry. We will find him for you and for the sake of getting closure."

While Rachel and I looked at each other, not sure what they were talking about, Drew walked over to Tim and Karen and talked to them for a while. I think they were discussing what to do.

I reached over to Rachel and squeezed her hand. Rachel tried to act normal, but I could tell she was upset and worried by the news…Nat was still missing. She looked like she was going to cry, and I wanted to, too. "Rach, let's stay positive," I said. "He's still missing. He isn't gone, thank God," I said, dreading and not wanting to say the word "dead". "If the team over there could get your father and some others out, especially since that was supposedly a very tight and dangerous operation, then they can find Nat."

"I know," Rach said, a tear ran down her cheek. "I missed him so much. When Drew moved down to Malibu to go to USC this semester, and Mom was getting on my nerves at home, I would always go over to Nat's place and we'll talk. He's so grown up for his age, Sum, and so wise. I mean he's only about two years older than us, but he's like a father figure to me more than Dad ever was. Plus I could talk to him about everything." Rach gulped. "Even about Ryan, you, or Astor."

I raised my eyebrows. "Me?" I licked my lips. "You talk about me to Nat?"

"Nothing bad, Summer, just about how he thinks Astor would feel about you being with Nat, and what to do to get Astor to notice me."

"Rach!" I almost laughed. "You do have a crush on Astor!"

"Doesn't every warm-blooded female in America?" Rachel asked.

"Yeah, true, but…"

"Don't worry, Astor still talks all the time about you. He's still worried about that stalker and checks to see if anyone's tried to break into the Academy again or if there is vandalism. He really cares about you, Summer," Rachel said seriously. "I'm a little jealous, but I realize I do like him because he cares about you. If he didn't, I would think he's the most heartless arrogant…"

I hugged Rach. If there was one thing, Rachel was loyal and got my back, crush on a major heartthrob or not.

"So Nat and you talk about me?" I asked again.

"Mostly Nat…he wanted to know how serious you were with Astor that one time Astor showed up at the Academy's Open House and Astor helped Drew cater it. He also wanted to know how you were doing when the Academy was vandalized. I mean, I know you and Nat are close, and he's probably the most self-confident guy I know, besides Drew, but sometimes, I feel as though when it comes to you, Nat had some deep insecurities. He would worship the ground you walk on, if you let him." Rachel took a deep breath. "Oh God, Summer, if anything bad happened to him, I would be devastated. Devastated. I'm closer to Nat than to Mom and Dad. Mom and Dad…they couldn't care less about me, but Nat…he always cared. He always did the right thing even if it meant he had to sacrifice his own happiness for everyone else."

Talking about Nat with Rachel brought back everything I loved about Nat, and I found myself dripping tears uncontrollably down my cheeks. My nose was stuffed up, and I couldn't breathe. I stood up and grabbed my purse. "Excuse me," I said quickly while I walked out of the room and quickly down the hall, looking for the ladies' room.

I was composing myself in front of the mirror in the ladies' room when the door opened, and the strategist Karen Waters walked in. I immediately wiped my cheeks with my hands, and said, "Hi."

"Hey," Karen said, coming towards me with her arms held out. Out of characteristic with her role at Donovan Dynamics, she gave me a quick hug and then stood back. She had a kind but serious expression on her face. "It's going to be alright," she said.

"I hope so," I replied. "I really hope so...Nat is...well, he's very special to me."

"I know," Karen said. She took a deep breath, looked away, and said, "He's a pretty great guy, isn't he? I've known him for a few years now, and he's always has been respectful, kind, spectacular, and incredibly bright. One of the smartest brains at Donovan Dynamics."

"Really?" I said. "You could tell in just a couple of years?" I asked.

"Oh, yes, quite a genius," Karen said. "He is pretty much the brains behind Donovan Dynamics' Cyber Security and Intelligence division. Everyone in that group working on this search was supervised by him at one time or another. Believe me, we want him back just as much as anyone."

"But he just started taking on his father's duties here," I said. "He has college, his mother's health, and other stuff to think about, let alone run divisions here."

"No, he's been doing so since he was a kid. He would spend his nights and weekends at the office poring over the computer, helping his father out. Like I said, he was a genius. I have every confidence that he was the one to get Mr. Donovan out safe and sound. Nat's a hero-type, too. He'd stay behind to make sure everything went smoothly. He wouldn't leave anyone behind. He's a real leader and team player. That is why everyone here, despite Nat's age, admire and look up to him. We will try our best to find him and bring him back."

"You mean Nat had been working here since Donovan Dynamics began?" I asked. Why was I so shocked? It was his father's company so of course he would be part of it, but somehow I was shocked. Nat knew a lot more about cyber security and intelligence than I've ever realized.

"Take heart in knowing Nat is no ordinary young man, Summer. He's very resourceful, bright, and capable of unbelievable things. Without him, Mr. Donovan could not have built Donovan Dynamics into what it is today...the world's largest and foremost private security corporation. Whatever is making him stay out of the picture must be something special." Karen looked at me quizzically. "You and Nat are close, as in more than friends?"

I nodded. "Had a crush on him since we were toddlers and then we finally got together this winter."

"Had any major fights with him?" Karen asked.

"No," I said, "we were getting along great before he left."

"Knowing how he is such a focused guy," Karen said, "it would take something very personal and deeply felt for him to disappear from the radar like that…I mean, now don't take this badly, Nat does have the means to communicate with us, if he choose to…but we haven't heard from him at all since he left."

"Why would he do that?" I asked.

"It makes me wonder, too," Karen said. "But looking at you, having met you, having seen you and Drew together, well…there is more than meets the eyes…" she raised her eyebrows in a question.

I gulped. Then it hit me what was clear and visible to Karen…Drew and I were passionately kissing each other in the lot outside of Donovan Dynamics right before meeting everyone for our first meeting. We were probably very visible for everyone to see. And the way Drew was so protective around me in front of everyone, it was clear he and I had something going on. I wanted to bang my head on the wall, thinking how awful something liked that looked, and of course, if I was Nat seeing the love of my life with my own brother, I would be heartbroken too. Not wanting to go back home to deal with that.

"I see," I said. "Well, if he could be here now, he would see how devastated and affected I am with him missing…how much I cared for and loved him. He would see that no matter what appears on the surface, things are not what they seem, and there is always a chance to work something out if we could only sit down to talk about it."

Karen nodded. "Point well-taken. Sounds like Nat didn't fall for some ordinary girl, too. Talking of which…" she looked at her watch. "If you stay here long enough or decide to come back tomorrow morning, we are hoping to see Mr. Donovan and the other hostage as they stop by."

"I'd like to see that," I said. However in my heart, I was dreading the meeting. For Mr. Donovan to come back safely while Nat was still missing and in danger made me angry with the unfairness of it. Nat did everything for his father, He helped step in for his father to care for his mother's mental illness. He stepped in to be more of a father figure to Rachel and Drew than his father, He helped covered for his father, kept his father's dirty secret of having an affair with his secretary from his mother until he finally told her, and now I found out Nat helped build up Donovan Dynamics from the start.

I was furious to think Nat gave up so much for his father, while his father was coming back safe and sound to Donovan Dynamics and to his mistress. I couldn't care less to see him now. Not when Nat was still missing.

"I'm sorry," I said, "I just realize I have to go back to Malibu tonight to take care of some things at home. Drew might be staying here, though. He could be here to see Mr. Donovan again. I'll be going back home with Rachel."

"Alright, Ms. Jones," Karen said. "That's perfectly alright. Life goes on, and of course you have other obligations. You should live your life, think of other things, do things outside of this so you wouldn't drive yourself insane with worry. Seriously, you should go back home to get back into your routines, go back to taking classes in college, teaching and running your acting classes, play volleyball than worry about this. There is nothing you could do at this point, Summer, but let us handle it. This is what we do, and we will do our very best."

I hugged Karen and said, "Thank you, this meant a lot."

Then I walked outside where Rachel was gesturing to me. She still had tears in her eyes, but she was surprisingly calm. "The jet's in the hangar, and my ride to the hangar is here. You want to come back to Malibu with me? All this waiting, wringing, doing nothing is driving me crazy. I have to get back to the Academy, do something else. I mean, I love Nat and all, but I feel so useless in that room while everyone is so busy in discussion planning some kind of Special Forces attack or rescue…something. Drew is right in the middle of it. I think he'll be here all night."

"I'll have to tell him I'm going with you," I said.

"Good, because from the looks of it, if you don't, you'll be sleeping on the couch in the lobby all night if you wait. He didn't even have time to wave me 'good-bye'. He nodded and went back to talking to the team. They are planning on getting some results tomorrow. They have no time for us right now, Summer. We might as well go home and wait to hear about some news tomorrow."

"Okay," I said heading into the boardroom. I peeked inside, and Drew was in the middle of a call, but he saw me. He got up and came to me, while holding his phone, and put his arm around me. I could see how badly he wanted to kiss me, but he didn't. "I'm going back to the Pad with Rach," I whispered. "I'll let you work. I'll be fine with Rach."

Drew nodded and watched me walk out of the boardroom while still on the phone. It was the first time he looked absolutely determined and dead serious about something. He was not the fun-loving Drew I knew last summer, but a man who was taking matters and his life into his own hands. For some reason, seeing him this determined to get his brother back home, despite their rivalry, made me so proud of him. It made me realize that no matter what his situation and relationship with Nat was like, he would survive and be fine with it.

Nat had told me about his dream regarding Drew. He had told me in great details one night after we made love at the Pad. It was his family's demon, the darkness that could haunt everyone in the house…those depressed feelings, those repressed emotions, the possibility of mental illness that could be passed down to either of the Donovans offsprings. Nat had dreamed of Drew seeing Nat and I making love and had been so depressed and devastated by that, so heartbroken that in his dream, Drew pulled the trigger that ended his life. Nat was shaking when he told me about that dream. He was so upset that he refused to touch me and make love to me or kiss me whenever he thought Drew was around us. He made that vow to me that he wouldn't show any pda towards me if he knew Drew was there. He kept that promise too. But now seeing this side of Drew, seeing how he handled all this, made me realize maybe just maybe we had underestimated Drew.

Chapter 11

Summer

I was jogging along the beach early in the morning that drew up against the Pad's back patio, when Rachel, in her curlers, black camisole and plaid shorts pajamas came running up to me.

Rach was now staying at the Pad full-time while she finished her internship at the Academy. Needless to say, I was happy to have her there with me. Just us girls. Without all the drama of the boys being there.

After we flew back to Malibu, she ordered pizza and Chinese food, and we ate and ate until we were agonizingly stuffed. Then we played music, watched *Mean Girls*, recited all the lines we loved in *Mean Girls*, and fell asleep in each other's arms. We were exhausted from worry, but being able to relive those carefree childhood days with Rachel had lifted our spirits, if only just for one night.

It was as though Aunt Sookie was back in our lives, telling us girls to live life to the fullest, to go after what we really wanted out of life and never look back. Never have regrets. Never apologize for being you. Being back in Malibu in Aunt Sookie's beach house calmed my soul, and made me realize how fortunate I was to have known all the special people who came into my life at different stages and points of my life…Aunt Sookie, Rachel, Nat, Drew, Astor, Nadine Donovan, and even Ryan. To me, it was fate that I have them in my life…if fate was to act again and separate one or any of them from my life; then there was a purpose for it, a purpose I couldn't see in the present, but will someday realize. Knowing this helped provide me with peace and tranquility in a sea of uncertainty. Knowing this helped me prepare for the news I was about to hear from Donovan Dynamics. Thank God, I had that strength. Thank God, Rachel was with me. If not, I would have collapse to the ground and have never wanted to get back up.

"Summer," Rachel said, "Summer!"

"Yeah, what?" I said slowing down my jog to a sudden halt. "What?"

Rachel's face was wet from crying. From heavy sobbing. "It's Nat..." she cried. "They sent a Special Forces team to find any trace of Nat," she cried. "He had helped Dad get out of whatever crime organization that had him. He was the one to get another hostage out. You wouldn't guess who it was..."

"Who?" I asked.

"Your mother," Rachel said. "Your mother was held by this crime organization she was investigating for the military. Then she went missing, and Dad made it a personal mission of his to find her. He promised Mom and Aunt Sookie he would do everything he could to find her."

My eyes probably shot out of my head with surprise. "Why didn't anyone tell me? Why didn't I know? It's my mother. Don't I have a right to know? I knew she was off on some kind of special assignment, so I didn't try to contact her, wanting her to focus on her mission, get it done, and come home, but this...Oh God...how long was she kept prisoner? Was she mistreated? Oh God...she was the military hostage your father was traveling back with...I should've stayed to see her!"

"Summer, she's okay; she's fine. They treated her well enough. She's exhausted but she will be making her way here tomorrow."

I put my hands to my face rubbing it out of nervous energy. "Thank God Mom is safe."

"Thanks to Nat," Rachel said, looking solemn. "He was a real hero, going there to get them out. He had to go into the headquarters of some criminal organization to do it, and..." Rachel gulped. "The Special Forces team Drew sent over last night found something. The men who was part of Nat's team had been killed. Nat was nowhere to be found nearby. But that crime ring had been known to wash away all traces of their crimes, including murder. I can't go into detail what they found of the team Nat had been with, but if Nat was with them, there would be barely anything left of him."

I fell to the ground, feeling the rush of sand meet my face and scraping it. My head was spinning, and I was seeing half the sky and half blurry darkness. Nat. Nat. Nat…he was dead.

Chapter 12

Nat

The deed had been done. I'm a bastard in so many ways for putting my loved ones through this grief. Rachel may forgive me one day…she's still considered my sister, but Summer, I won't blame her for hating me forever. Perhaps it was better that she hated me, than hold some kind of hope out for me…that I would return to her, make her happy, and live happily ever after with her.

Than for her to find out the truth.

*****

Lamar, an FBI giant with muscles everywhere, packed up the computer equipment from the van securely and loaded it into an unidentifiable vehicle. It was the last of the valuable hardware that had to go to the lab for data analysis.

"Good job, Rookie," Lamar's booming deep voice said, while he slapped me on the back hard enough to make my teeth chatter. "We have the evidence we need to bring a suit against the ring. Then you can send that mother fucking psycho to prison where he belongs. No more tormenting young women with blackmailed photos of them, no more stalking celebrities and hacking into their accounts. Your girl could rest assure we got one of her biggest cyber-bullies. Or at least we will. How did you put two and two together? That was genius by the way…"

"When I went into the computer of their headquarters searching for a code, I found the name of a man who had been stalking Summer and also Summer's Aunt Sookie. He seemed to know too much about Summer and had access to very personal photos…I knew he was connected to some kind of cybercriminal activity that was bigger than an one-person operation. Well, bingo, his name popped up in the database on this crime ring's computer as one of their own. Sloane, Wilma, KazuKen, Celi-hag, BunnyMuff, were all part of the illegal and criminal cyber-bullying ring that used blackmail to extort celebrities and famous authors, musicians, schools like Aunt Sookie Acting Academy for money or they will post lies, false rumors, photo shopped fake photos, and accusations of fake awards, fake credentials on the internet. They did that to Summer and tried to do that with Aunt Sookie, apparently. But as seemingly innocent as they seem, using young girls' photos as their supposed fake identities, they really were part of a larger crime ring."

"Why Summer and why the Acting Academy?" Lamar asked.

"Because of revenge…Summer's mother found evidence of their criminal activity once and had reported them. These cyber criminals were ruthless, went after anyone associated with Major Jones…meaning Summer and Aunt Sookie. Of course Summer also got attacked for getting into the public eye when she dated that pretty boy actor Astor Fairway."

"Well, good job, and glad we could put your genius cyber-crime solving mind to work for us. It was about time we found this to bring about justice." Lamar looked into the van and noted that it was completely cleaned out.

"What next?" I asked.

"We torch the van so there are no traces of this ever happening. We've already masked the scene at the headquarters to appear as though all the men who accompanied you as part of your Special Forces team, were killed."

"They weren't?" I asked, the relief clearly running across my face.

"No," Lamar said. "When you decided to head back to a part of the fence close to the area Tito was trying to get through, and rammed it with the van to create an opening large enough for any of the guys to go through, before you headed out as fast as you could, that created the escape and diversion they needed to escape, scatter, and hide into the forest."

"Where are they now?" I asked. "Are they still in the forest?"

"No, these men you hired are the most elite of the elite. They've been in far more dangerous missions and lived to face others. They did what they had to do, escaped, and probably went their separate ways afterwards, never to meet up again. I would do the same thing."

"Is that what I'm supposed to do now?" I asked. "I was part of that team. Do I go back to being a normal college student again?"

"Nat," Lamar said, leading me away from the van and to the opposite side of the garage where there was a simple, no-frills beat-up looking silver 1998 Honda Civic. "Actually, Nat, you will still be a college student, only a normal one...one with college tuition worries, school loans, dorm-room living, and girl troubles...Because you were in this mission, not only acting for your father's company, but also for the FBI, you could not assume your old identity. It would be too dangerous, for you and for anyone you care about. That criminal ring had your face and name snapshot as soon as you entered the premises. They could find Nat Donovan. Unless he disappears. The rest of your team…they knew the dangers, too. They've disappeared. Now Nat Donovan has to disappear, too. You will be another college student, so at least you could finish college and move on with your life, but not Nat Donovan."

I swallowed. This was hard to take. I knew this mission was dangerous, but I didn't think about the consequences afterwards, if I survived. "Who will I be?"

"A student attending USC on a scholarship. A film major. You're also a player who goes through girls like candy. We can color your hair blonde, put blue contacts into your eyes…this is the car you'll be driving. This life is completely different than Nat Donovan's. What do you think?"

"This is the way it has to be? Would anyone in my family know? What about my mother…she needs caring, would someone watch her for me? Summer…oh God, what about Summer, could I see her again?"

Secrets of the Fall (Donovan Brothers #2: Loving Summer #3)

Lamar, who looked and seemed younger than his forty years, shook his head. "Your brother Drew knows you're alive. But he thinks it's because you left on your own accord, that you wanted to distance yourself from Summer, considering you may be blood—related to her. He knows you're alive, but won't reveal it because he personally have some stake in having you disappear or declared as dead."

I could not believe what Lamar was saying, Drew would want me out of the picture alright, to be with Summer. I just didn't think he'd actually want me dead.

"Everyone else believe the story the new ex-Special Forces team Drew and Donovan Dynamics sent last night, gave…that they found pieces of the men from your team left at the headquarters, and that you were probably part of that, too."

I bent over to keep from hyperventilating; I was knocked clear out of breath. I was dead to my family now. I was dead to Summer. To never be able to touch or hold her again. To never be able to kiss her again, despite whether or not we were tabooed from ever being together. I didn't even know if I was Aunt Sookie's son.

All this was too much to handle. I could handle everything else, but losing Summer was the one thing I couldn't. She was my weakness, my Achilles heel. The one constant in my crazy abnormal life. How would I deal with seeing her but not being able to have her?

"Nat," Lamar said. "Your transporter's here. He'll take you across the border. Then you'll see this same exact car parked at the parking garage near Pike's Market. From there, you can drive to San Francisco and on down the California highway to USC where you're set up with a dorm."

"Will I ever have my life back again?" I asked. "Will I ever get to return to being Nat Donovan?"

"That's a sound iffy, Nat. For now, to keep yourself safe, and to be able to work for us to get this crime ring completely busted, you would have to be this other person. This is the way for you to still help Summer out, and still be close enough to her."

"But not as myself," I said. "When could I be myself with her?"

"When we bust this cybercrime ring, and bring all of them to justice so you, Summer, and Summer's mother are safe."

"This is going to devastate Summer. I have a hard time putting her through this...she just lost her aunt for God's sake."

Lamar looked me squarely in the face. "Then do what you need to do to put yourself at ease with this. What do you need to do to find some kind of closure?"

I said, "Do you have a pen and paper?"

Lamar brought out a briefcase from his vehicle and opened it revealing stationery of all kinds as well as different types of pens, pencils, and writing utensils. "For my 5 year-old daughter, but also for our line of work. Clean up, disguises, espionage."

I took a nice fine point blue ink pen and an ivory linen pad of paper and began writing. When I was done in less than five minutes, I handed it to Lamar. "Can I make this look like it's been through a lot to get to her?" I asked.

"Easy," Lamar said. "I'm a master of disguises, change identities, and appearances. This is a piece of cake."

"Good," I said, "because Summer would probably see through it if it wasn't done right."

"Well…we've fooled the crime ring you're dead already. Now are you ready to be resurrected as someone new?"

"As ready as I could be," I answered. "When I thought about the possibility of being blood related to Summer, my life already was forfeit."

Epilogue

<u>Summer</u>

The letter I held in my hands was bent and torn, patched up a few times with tape, and looked as though it went through some rough times. If only it could talk, I bet there would be a good story with how it got to me. If it could talk, it would be able to answer all the questions that I had that came up as soon as I saw who had sent it.

Nat.

When? How? Why did it take so long to get to me?

Those were the first questions that came up.

Then came many more…

Nat's Letter to Summer

My Perfect Summer,

I hope you will and can forgive me.

I never meant to hurt you, but sometimes we do things because we thought it was the best or only way out.

I don't know where to begin. But if you are holding this letter in your hands, then I know you already have a sense of what this is about.

Again, I am writing you a letter not because I am old-fashioned, but because this time, it was necessary. It was the only way I can get word out to you that I am okay. That I am alive.

Secrets of the Fall (Donovan Brothers #2: Loving Summer #3)

I can't have you suffering over grief for me, thinking I was dead. I am in the sense I could not be with you in more ways than one.

I will always love you, Summer. You are the world to me, but circumstances have changed. I don't know if I will ever be the same Nat as you loved. If I could return to be the Nat that you could be with. Sometimes in the line of duty, you are forced to do things that you would not be proud of. There were a few things I had to do in order to get the job done. But I did it, and because I did, my father will be on his way back home.

Will I come home soon? It depends. I don't know when or if so that's why I'm writing you this letter.

Please go on living life to the fullest as you've always have. Go on and be as happy as you can be, and don't put your life on hold for me to be happy. I know how you feel about Drew, and I know how Drew feels about you. With me no longer there for you, please turn to Drew for support. He knows why I'm doing this, and he knows how to comfort you best, as well as how to protect you.

Life is too short to wait for love. I am so grateful for the chance we had together. I take those memories with me everywhere I go, but it is now time for me to let you go, and for you to let me go. I love you with all my heart so I am letting you go to fulfill your destiny, as I am doing so now.

Love Your Nat in Shining Armor for Always

*****

As I re-read the letter over and over again, I felt somewhat of an elation from reading this battered and torn letter. Relief that Nat was indeed alive, but sad and angry that he would not be returning to me, that he or whoever it was behind his disappearance had allowed me to experience such devastating grief over him.

It had been a week since Rachel told me the news about Nat's death, and I cried my heart and soul out for him.

But today, looking at this letter, I couldn't cry any longer. I was cried out. Now it was replaced with fury.

I called Drew and asked him to meet me at the Pad as soon as he could. Since Nat's death, he practically lived there after he drove back down to Malibu. He stayed with Rachel and I at the Pad every day, and when Rachel was out teaching a class or going to auditions now that Astor had found her an agent, Drew would sneak up to me to kiss me and make love to me. We would sleep together every night, and wake up hot for each other again.

Knowing that Nat was dead, Drew told me, gave me closure. I was allowed to move on, to date other guys, to be with Drew in all ways.

I let Drew comfort me, to make love to me, to have me all over him, to give myself freely to him because of this closure. All because Nat was gone.

Now I knew Nat was alive. He gave me his blessings for me to be with Drew, but he was alive. And the worse part of it, Drew knew it. He knew and let me suffer through the grief, and even used it to cement our relationship together.

I was furious.

I felt like a fool, played by Drew and Nat.

When Drew walked through the door of the Pad a half hour after I texted him to meet, he had a smile on his face, a big happy dopey smile that only a man happy in love could have. He also had a bouquet of gigantic red roses which he presented to me.

"Summer," he said, grabbing me around the waist, lifting me in the air, and swinging me. "I love you so much, Summer, I want you to come out to dinner with me. A special restaurant by the beach, candle-lit dinner, music…"
He brought out a box that had a very familiar color – Tiffany blue.

I immediately thought of Astor when I saw the Tiffany box.

"This is for you, Sum…I noticed you love these type of things."

"No Drew, you don't have to," I said, touched by his sweetness, but still furious with his deception.

Drew opened the box and took out the jewelry inside. "I'm not Astor or Nat," Drew said. "This piece of jewelry was custom-made and different than the other ones you have."

He showed me a beautiful diamond tennis bracelet with little gold loops for diamond charms. There was a starfish, a princess crown, a pirate, a theatrical mask, a jet, and pancakes all in diamond gems. It was beautiful so beautiful I was distracted from what I wanted to say to him.

"It's beautiful," I said. "Thank you."

"Not as beautiful as you, Summer. You make me so happy and so complete, I've never been so happy before."

My heart sank. I loved Drew so much, and I enjoyed being with him, and wanted to still, but knowing what I did about Nat, I had to confront him for lying to me.

"Drew," I said. "I received something strange but very precious and important in the mail today."

I held up the envelope and then showed him the letter. His guilt-ridden face and loss of words was all I needed to know he knew about Nat being alive. But why?

"I'm sorry Summer," Drew said. "So very sorry that you had to find out this way. You must really hate me right now."

I couldn't even answer him. How dare he let me believe Nat was dead when he knew all along he wasn't. How dare he make me cry myself to sleep every night for weeks, knowing Nat was alive. He watched me at my most vulnerable, at my most devastated, yet he knew Nat was alive. Yet he took advantage of the situation.

I was furious beyond words. Finally, I said through clenched teeth, "Drew, get the hell out. I never want to see you again, and your lying face."

With that, I shoved the bracelet back to him, pushed him out the door, and slammed it shut. Then I felt my world collapse on me...but this time, there was no one around me to pick me up off the ground ...only myself. Life was going to become much simpler.

Secrets of the Fall (Donovan Brothers #2: Loving Summer #3)

Summer, Drew, Nat, Rachel, and Astor's story continues in

Book 3 of the Loving Summer Series

Lasting Summer (Loving Summer Series #3)

Release Date to Be Determined

Sign Up for the New Releases Newsletter to find out when:

Kailingowbooks(at)aol(dot)com

Kailin Gow

The Truth Behind the Donovan Brothers Series and Cyber-bullying

When I first became an author and began publishing books in the YA genre, I faced my first incidence of cyber-bullying.

An anonymous blogger (whom it was revealed was someone working in the publishing industry, did not like independently-published authors and was also working for an author as their agent who saw me as a rival) began posting lies, accusations, and threats to certain authors and bloggers who were popular and doing well at the time. I was amongst that group. As it went along, the posts and attacks became more and more bizarre and far-fetched.

Cyber-bullying behavior is psychopathic behavior. When a person is relentless in attacking someone online or even in person for any reason which they can talk themselves into justifying, it becomes psychopathic and dangerously violent.

Secrets of the Fall (Donovan Brothers #2: Loving Summer #3)

Cyber-bullying is slowly being recognized as criminal. By helping concerned citizens and organizations set up measures on their site, at their schools, and internet presence where it discourage cyber-bullying behavior rather than encourage it, I am proud to take part in bringing that awareness.

Cyber-bullying may seem harmless or is protected under the wide umbrella of free speech, but it can kill. People have died from it.

I am very blessed that I have the support of many incredible people and organizations who have stood by me.

Credible organizations with stellar reputations such as CBS TV News, Amazon.com, IMDB.com, the O.C. Register, The World Journal, Huffington Post, and top 15 National radio shows have written about and featured me...organizations that are unbiased in their reporting.

Most of all, I have the support of many loyal readers like you.

Kailin Gow

I feel blessed to be able to share Summer, Drew, Nat, Rachel, and Astor's stories with you, and am so thrilled and still so touched that you love these characters as much as I do.

We are getting close to the end of this series, and I want to hear from you to help me determine whether you would like to see more and who.

If you would like to have more books in the Loving Summer Series or a spin-off, let me know by sending me an email.

kailingowbooks@aol.com

THANK YOU!!!

<u>Excerpt from:</u>

Saving You

Saving Me

kailin gow

Kailin Gow

Prologue

I'm standing here, holding a key; the one Daggers had given me before he left. "It's the key to my heart," he had said, pressing it into my hands. "You have my heart already, you might as well have everything else," he said softly as he kissed away my tears. He pulled me in close to his chest and held me tight. "We've come a long ways, baby. You and I. But we still have some distance to cover, hurdles to jump, if you want to." He laughed his soft gentle Daggers laugh that always sent flutters to my stomach. "I'm a many-layered SOB, a real messed up nut job, who others have given up on, yet you…you continue to peel away the layers." He played with my hair and kissed my forehead. I sighed. My multi-layered Daggers. Each layer more intriguing than the last, each one bringing me closer to the edge of no return.

"I want to peel away those layers," I protested. "I want to know who you are; deep down, if you'll let me."

Daggers closed his eyes for a moment and inhaled sharply. "I know, Sam, and I've been fighting it. If you knew what's really hidden behind all those layers, you'd stay away from me, as far away from me as possible." He opened his eyes to look at me earnestly. "You deserve to know, though. And I'm giving you that chance. With the key...the key to my safe deposit box. But once you know, there's no going back."

Chapter 1

Two Months Earlier

Monday

"Sammy! Sammy!" Nydia ran to me before she headed into her kindergarten class.

"What?" I asked, kneeling down so she could walk into my arms where I automatically pulled her in for a hug. I touched her braid and playfully used it to tickle her.

"Stop Sammy!" Nydia giggled.

"Not going to until you tell me what's up, baby," I giggled with her. Except for her green eyes, that mirrored mine...the exact same shade of deep green as our mother's, she looked like a smaller and cuter version of Dad with her dark hair and pale skin.

Mom's green eyes peered at me from her sweet heart-shaped face. "Are you going to pick me up today or is Mom?"

I sighed. "I wish I could, pip squeak, but I have school stuff." I squished my face into as sad of a face as possible. "I'm sorry, baby, but Mom's going to have to pick you up like she always does."

"But I want you to," Nydia said. "Not Mom."

"Nydia," I said gently. "Mom loves picking you up." I tugged at her dark braids and whispered into her ears. "Besides, you promised to keep an eye on her," I said smiling. "For me."

Nydia smiled her secret smile. "Alright, Sammy. For you."

I touched the tip of her little nose with the tip of my finger, "I love you."

"I love you too," Nydia said.

"Now go in before you're late," I said standing up.

"Okay," Nydia hugged me again. "But I hate the way Mommy smells sometimes."

I cringed inwardly. "Me, too, pip squeak. Me, too." I pulled back from her hug and watched her walk into class. I was not going to let her see me upset. This morning was perfect. My life was perfect, and when I think about how sweet it is to be blessed with a perfect little girl as my baby sister, I thank my lucky stars for helping me see things will only get better. I pushed the negative sad thoughts out of my mind. I could not dwell on it. It did no one any good to dwell on it. I had to be stronger than that, to think of better things. Because no matter how bad it gets at home, I have my little sister who will always be there for me, and I for her.

As soon as she walked in, and I waved good-bye, I ran to my car, and drove as fast as I could to school. My meeting with our school counselor was early this morning, and I did not want to be late.

I pulled into the school parking lot, got out of the car, and ran awkwardly in my boots and skirt.

"Hey Sam," Gina from my English class called. "Happy belated birthday. The big 1-8. You're legal now! Whoo hoo!"

"Thanks," I laughed. "You'll be there soon."

"Sam," John Wrangler, a thin but tall guy from my debate class strode up to me and said, "Hear from the colleges, yet?"

I rolled my eyes. "It's still early. I have some time to get in what I need to boost my chances for acceptance. You?"

"Not yet, too. I'd thought you'd hear by now. All the schools would want you," he said nervously.

"Yeah right," I snorted. "My chances for getting in are just like everyone else's. Speaking of…I really have to get to my meeting with Dr. Green." I waved. "Good luck!"

I ran the rest of the way into the building to the offices, and into Dr. Green's office and sat down right when the clock on her wall struck 8:30 am.

Dr. Karen Green looked up from the paper in front of her. "Sam, let's get down to it. You've had a fine academic career at Cliffside Academy. A 4.2 grade point average will help you get in along with your high SAT scores, but you need something else to get a scholarship, too," Dr. Green said, tapping her long pink fingernails across the plain manila file folder labeled "Samantha Sullivan."

Inwardly I sighed. What else could I do to try to make it inevitable I could get a scholarship to Stanford? I'd worked so hard just to get the academic record I had. "Do you have any suggestions?" I asked my guidance counselor for three years. Dr. Green, with her messy brown shoulder-length hair, big hoop plastic yellow earrings, and black and white striped dress did not look like a counselor. The only thing that looked counselor-like on her was her smart chick glasses, the kind hot librarians wore. Who would've guessed funky Dr. Green was the best high school guidance counselor in all of Orange County, California.

"As a matter of fact, I do," she said getting up and walking over to a small black and white striped fabric-covered push-pin bulletin board hanging on top of a set of black metal-lock cabins. She reached over and unpinned a brochure from the board and handed it to me.

I scanned it quickly, before looking back up at her.

"Well?" she asked.

"It's a brochure for a teen call center," I said. "Sawyer House - a place where teens can call to talk about whatever problems they have without being judged." I looked quizzically at Dr. Green. Why did she hand me this brochure? Did she think I needed help without waiting to say it outright?

"What do you think about volunteering there as a peer counselor, Sam?"

I swallowed. "I've never done anything like that before."

"Then it'll be a real experience for you," Dr. Green said, a glint in her brown eyes. "Look, Sam, I wouldn't suggest this to you if I didn't think you can handle it. You're an exemplary student, you've been class president of the junior class last year, you're active in your father's church, you're the school student ambassador...you're one of the most mature students in school."

Yeah, I also just turned eighteen years old so technically, I was a little older than my peers in high school. I blushed with Dr. Green's assessments of me. It wasn't something I strived to do. Being involved in school was something I'd done all my life, given I was a pastor's kid, and I had always been involved in one social activity or another. And the reason why everyone thought I was mature for my age...well, that was complicated, more complicated than I wanted to delve into.

"Um, Dr. Green," I said. "I don't know about this...I mean, I have a few things going on right now, and you've just said I'm already involved in some activities. Surely that's enough to get me that extra edge to get into the college of my choice?"

"Stanford's very competitive to get in, Sam. All the applicants have grade point averages like yours. All of them have a few extracurricular activities. What you need to get into the same psychology program I went through as an undergrad, you need something like this." Dr. Green smiled. "Really, Sam, I thought you would've done something like this already. You're perfect for it." She took the brochure out of my hands and reached for her phone. "In fact, I'm going to recommend you to them right now. I know the director of the center, and she'll be delighted to have you." Dr. Green punched some numbers on her phone and waited a few seconds. Then she was talking. "Gail Reynolds, please," she said. "Tell her, it's Dr. Karen Green from Cliffside Academy." She looked over at me, smiling a "trust me, I know you'll love this" smile.

I sat back and watched her, trying to look interested. As she waited to be connected to the center's director, I glanced out the window of her office and into the hallway of the school administration office, trying to avoid her eyes, in case she saw the doubt in them.

It was a momentous glance, something I'm sure would have counted as one of the biggest moments of my life against which every other moment in my young life would pale. I did a double take as my eyes made contact with the coolest ice blue eyes I'd ever seen, and they belonged to Collins McGregor - the youngest mogul music producer featured on the cover of the latest issue of People Magazine. I felt my mouth dropped, but quickly recovered when Collins McGregor broke his gaze and a pink flush went up his cheeks.

He was better-looking than his photos, and I couldn't help staring at him, from his slightly messy wavy blonde hair, his sculpted cheeks and full sensual rocker lips, his tall and lean muscular body to his John Lobb-clad leather shoes. Dressed in a crisp white shirt and a silk small-patterned herringbone pale blue tie that matched his eyes, he looked every inch like a confident cocky young music mogul. Looking further down his tall and muscular frame was another story. Snug well-worn denim jeans hung off his hips in a sexy way that showed off powerful muscular legs and a tight butt. An expensive Italian black leather motorcycle jacket finished the ensemble. He was the picture of a hot bad boy music mogul. In person, he was gorgeous and stylish, exuding a confidence that permeated the room. Collins McGregor may be a music mogul, but he had the look and presence of a rock star. There was definitely something about him that kept me mesmerized. What was Collins McGregor doing at Cliffside Academy?

"Sam?" Dr. Green's voice interrupted my almost naughty thoughts of Collins.

I whipped my face so quickly from staring at Collins McGregor to Dr. Green's questioning face, I almost had whiplash. "Yes," I muttered, looking first at my hands and then at Dr. Green.

"Well," she said smiling. "You're in. You start this week. They had a peer volunteer who had to quit because she had to go back to college. They're understaffed and could really use your help."

"So when do I start?" I asked, shaking images of Collins McGregor out of my head.

"This Friday. They'll give you the orientation first and start you off with a practice call," Dr. Green said. "That's what Gail told me. You should get a packet in the mail in a few days with all the information." Dr. Green smiled a big Cheshire cat smile. "So, what do you think?"

I threw up my hands and shrugged. "I'll give it a try, Dr. Green. Thank you for getting me in so fast. I'm sure if you hadn't been involved, I wouldn't be starting this Friday."

"Oh, it's nothing," Dr. Green said. "I really think you have it in you to do this, Sam. You have to let me know how it goes…" She stood up, and walked to the door, signifying the end of our meeting. I stood up, smoothed out my navy pleated miniskirt, my soft pink ruffled blouse, and tucked my long wavy dark hair that came loose around my face, behind my ears, and walked out.

"Oh, wait," Dr. Green's voice called. I turned around, and she handed me the young adult center's brochure. I raised the brochure and nodded, turning around to head back outside. "Oh, Sam!" Dr. Green called. She walked towards me with my white cardigan. "You forgot this."

"Thank you," I said. Now I was going to be late for class if I didn't hurry out. I rushed out and bumped face first into something hard. When did a wall get put up outside the counselor's office? Then I lost my balance and landed on my butt, everything flying out of my hands as I tried to stop myself from falling harder.

Kailin Gow

Other Series from theEDGEbooks.com

Saving You Saving Me

    Aspiring psychiatrist and high school Valedictorian Samantha (Sam) Sullivan falls for a deeply troubled young man named Daggers during a crisis call at her watch, which leads to the unraveling of her perfect world.

Now Available!

CANVAS

I'm a 19 year old tattoo artist who works for my dad at his tattoo parlor that sits outside the studios where they're filming one of the most anticipated films, and the lead actor who is a sexy beast walks in one day to ask me to help him cover up a tattoo he'd gotten for a past love. They're beginning to film the movie, and he needs to do nude and sex scenes, so he comes running into the tattoo parlor one day when my dad is gone, and asks to get the tattoo he has removed or covered right down there. He strips, and since there's no one else to do his tattoo, I work on him for hours. I'm embarrassed at first to be touching him, but then realized he was having pain. He was also very turned on. I didn't know what to think of it, except that he was turned on by me, and a few days afterwards, wanted to see me. I've never dated an actor before, let alone a movie star in one of the hottest films, where all the women wanted him, yet here he is in my parlor, wanting me.

New NA series from Kailin Gow

Coming March 2014

Being His First

By
TJ Holly

She was his college English tutor, and he was her student…still in high school, and a foreign exchange student, living at her parents' home for the semester.

Their attraction was instant, but could it be more?

Coming February 2014

Kailin Gow

All for Amelia

By
AK Christian

He'd do anything to have Amelia, even if it meant
getting in too deep.

Coming in Spring 2014

Weigh in on LOVING SUMMER!

Which Team are You On? Still Team Drew or Team Nat or even Team Astor? Who should Summer End Up With? Weigh in and Help the author decide:

Team Drew

Team Nat

Team Astor

Vote on theEDGEbooks.com's
Loving Summer Poll

Kailin Gow

Find Out What Happens to Nat, Drew, Rachel, and Summer in the next Loving Summer book:

Lasting Summer

Release Date To Be Determined.

Sign up at theEDGEbooks.com to get notice of when Lasting Summer will be released.

OTHER BOOKS FROM KAILIN GOW

The FROST Series

The PULSE Series

Wicked Woods Series

Desire Series

Steampunk Scarlett Series

The Fire Wars Series

Fade Series

Circus of Curiosities

You & Me Trilogy

Never Say Never Series

Alchemists Academy Series

Wordwick Games Series

Phantom Diaries Series

Kailin Gow

Beautiful Beings Series

Stoker Sisters Series

And More!

VISIT KAILIN'S WEBSITE to learn about new releases, the most awesome contests and parties, what Kailin and friends are doing in the community, workshops and events Kailin will be at and more at:

http://www.kailingow.com

http://kailingow.wordpress.com

and

on Twitter at: @kailingow

KAILIN GOW'S 18+ Adult Romance Books
Newsletter

Are you over 18? Would you like to know more
about Kailin's books for adults and new adults?

Sign up for her newsletter at:

kailingowbook(at)aol(dot)com

Thank you for reading! – Kailin

www.ingramcontent.com/pod-product-compliance
Lightning Source LLC
Chambersburg PA
CBHW061144170626

46809CB00003B/979